Acknowledgments and Thanks

Many thanks to my God and my family for support and love beyond measure.

THE MAD AMERICAN

BOOK 2

DAY OF RECKONING

Skip Coryell

Published by White Feather Press. (www.whitefeatherpress.com)

ISBN 978-1-61808-213-8

Cover design by Phillip Coryell
Front cover brick texture ©shutterstock.com/ By Valentin Agapov
Front photo ruined city ©shutterstock.com/ By Design Projects

White Feather Press

Reaffirming Faith in God, Family, and Country!

Books by Skip Coryell

We Hold These Truths
Bond of Unseen Blood
Church and State
Blood in the Streets
Laughter and Tears
RKBA: Defending the Right to Keep and Bear Arms
Stalking Natalie
The God Virus
The Shadow Militia
The Saracen Tide
The Blind Man's Rage
Civilian Combat - The Concealed Carry Book
Jackpine Strong
Concealed Carry for Christians
The Covid Chronicles: Surviving the Upgrade
The Covid Chronicles: Surviving the Apocalypse
The Covid Chronicles: Surviving the Solstice
The Mad American - Judgment Day
The Mad American - Day of Reckoning
Sunrise Reflections: Finding Hope in Hard Times
Self Defense Scenarios: Staying Alive in a
Dangerous World

From the author

July 5th, 2022

Book 2 of *The Mad American* is about transition. How do we transition from a world of law and order, to a world of chaos and violence? I have to think that for most of us, the meek, the kind, the gentle, that it will be a difficult change, and that many of us will be unable to survive a society where the law of the jungle reigns supreme. In some cases it will happen quickly, perhaps even over night.

We are used to orderly transactions. We pull into the gas pump and if there's a line, then we wait patiently for our turn. When the power is out for a few hours, then the streetlight remains dark, and everyone cooperates by treating it like a 4-way stop. We know that if we take advantage of the system, there will be a price to pay; perhaps a traffic ticket or maybe even a more severe police response. Society has rules and there is a price to pay for breaking them.

But imagine a world where you dial nine-one-one, and you get a busy signal, or, worse yet, there is no dial tone and all communications are dead. That is a plausible scenario. What will happen then? What happens when the evil among us are no longer restrained? What happens when they are rewarded for killing, stealing and destroying? Very few of us want that world, and many of us would not survive it.

And I wonder ... *what about me*? What would I do in a situation where my family is starving and I have nothing to give them? Will I break into a store to feed my 10-year-old little girl or will I let her slowly starve to death in my arms as we both die?

Of course, that's part of the reason that I prep in the first place, so I won't have to watch my family die, but that begs another question. In a lawless scenario, am I willing to kill a starving human being, a father like myself, because he's breaking into my store room to feed his dying children? That's a tough call, but one that would have to be made.

These are disquieting images but they are the reality in this story, indeed, in most apocalyptic fiction. When people are faced with extreme societal change, they are forced to either adapt or die. But how does one adapt and survive while still maintaining human dignity, kindness and respect for others? Is it even possible?

Those are some of the questions I hope to answer by writing this story. My characters will be thrust into intolerable chaos and mayhem. And they will answer the question: *What is the price of my humanity?*

Thanks for reading my story. I hope you enjoy it and learn more about your own existence.

– Skip Coryell

> *Day of reckoning - A time when the consequences of a course of mistakes or misdeeds are felt.*
>
> *—Merriam Webster*

For Sara, my dear wife,
whom I love and fight for.

And to my children
and my grandchildren.

What has gone before…

In book one of this series, *The Mad American: Judgment Day*, Marvin Tubbs is the host and creator of a popular, syndicated radio show called, *The Mad American*. During the show, Americans from all walks of life call in to vent their frustrations about all facets of America and their lives. Marvin just listens patiently and seldom gives advice.

But Marvin's life changes when he meets a small-time podcaster named Matt Robbins. Matt's show is called *The Happy Prepper* and caters to those who are prepping for full-scale societal collapse or other short-term societal interruptions.

After meeting Matt, Marvin suspects that he needs a plan B, just in case society does turn sour, so he hires Matt to set up a bug-out location for him. During the course of his services, Matt meets and falls in love with Marvin's sister-in-law, Samantha.

Unfortunately, this budding romance is interrupted when North Korea, Iran, Russia and China all conspire in a coordinated attack on the United States.

At the end of book 1, Marvin, and his wife, Alexandra, have just fled Seattle on the way to their bug-out location in Pigeon Creek, Idaho where Matt lives. They watch in the rear-view mirror of their car as their Seattle home is consumed by the flames of a nuclear blast, along with several other major, American cities.

Meanwhile, back in Pigeon Creek, Samantha is helping Matt recover from a recent bear attack as they watch the world implode from the relative safety of a hospital bed. Will Marvin and Alexandra reach their bug-out location safely? Will Matt and Samantha be able to help them?

And thus, the story begins where it left off. I am proud to give you ... *The Mad American: Day of Reckoning!*

37 A furious squall came up, and the waves broke over the boat, so that it was nearly swamped. 38 Jesus was in the stern, sleeping on a cushion. The disciples woke him and said to him, "Teacher, don't you care if we drown?" 39 He got up, rebuked the wind and said to the waves, "Quiet! Be still!" Then the wind died down and it was completely calm.

Mark 4:37-39 (NIV)

PROLOGUE

Washington DC

YEARS AGO THERE WAS A POLI-
tician who tried to root out corruption from
the US Government and to end the selfish,
perpetuation of greed and oligarchy of power. He promised to drain the swamp. There was a terrible series of battles, and, in the end, the swamp monsters destroyed him,
tearing him limb from limb along with anyone who sup-
ported him, reasserting their stranglehold over America.
But then something happened that they had not intended.
Where the anti-politician had failed, the Iranians, with
the help of several low-yield nuclear devices, succeeded.
And, in one blinding flash of sightless and thoughtless
power, the swamp was irradiated, vaporized ... gone.

And now, just one day later, many of America's larg-
est cities rested calmly in radioactive rubble. Where there
had once been nightly riots and protests about police
brutality, systemic racism, and the unfair disposition of

wealth, there was now only ... silence. And not just for a day, but for a thousand years to come.

From that day forward, that particular point in time became known quite simply as ... 'The Day.' In general conversation, people would ask one another questions like "What did you do before The Day?" or "Before The Day I was quite rich. I owned three factories and had a vacation house in Key West." But after The Day, everything changed. It was as if God Himself had reached down, seeing that humanity had strayed hopelessly off course, and had pressed the reset button like only He could.

At first, as the power ceased to flow, and the screen grew dim, there was a general shock that manifested itself in silence and awe. Most people with even a modicum of common sense were suddenly reminded of one simple fact: "He's God and I'm not."

The polarization that had begun years before grew more potent and frenzied. People chose sides according to their natures. The evil became more ruthless. The good became more committed.

But as the silence began to fade, and the realization that this was a new era set in, that civilization and accountability would not be returning anytime soon, the evil, that had always been scattered loosely among us, began to gel and knit and form more closely together. They became more potent, more brazen, filled with power and boldness. At first the evil was random and scattered, but then, as the chaos continued and showed no signs of abatement, leaders sprang up and the strongest among them seized the day, and, the once controllable evil became overwhelming. It seethed and raged like a consuming fire that spread across the land, starting in the broken cities, filled with illness and starvation. Then, as resources grew scarce, the evil, like an infection, had no choice but to spread or die, always seeking out fresh, healthy tissue, then promptly feeding upon it and causing more death.

The good people who still remained were but a remnant. They were meek and kind by nature, but were forced to change if they were to survive. Those who adapted ... survived. Those who held on to the civilization of the old world perished quickly in a pool of their own blood.

But there were a few, a chosen few, strong in character and heart, who rose above the rest and asked the question: "What world should we rebuild?" They balanced kindness with justice; generosity with power. And they quickly learned that sheep-like compliance was a luxury they could no longer afford. As children they were taught that good always triumphed over evil, but, in this new age, they began to realize that good could only win when it was pure of heart and incredibly strong.

> *For evil plays by rules of its own*
> *making, and the rules constantly change*
> *to suit them.*

So, the second battle of the age began. The good ... the evil. And only one could win.

31 Get rid of all bitterness, rage and anger, brawling and slander, along with every form of malice. 32 Be kind and compassionate to one another, forgiving each other, just as in Christ God forgave you.

Ephesians 4:31-32 (NIV)

CHAPTER 1

Eastern Idaho

THE SECRET SERVICE AGENT took President Thornton to the back of the C-130 where the cargo door was already lowered. There was a lot of wind and noise, so Roger Thornton couldn't hear much of what Agent Bareman was telling him. Roger just nodded his head helplessly.

Just then General Ashby walked into the cargo bay area and yelled to the president. "Mr. President, the third engine just quit. Have you ever jumped out of an airplane before?"

The president scowled unhappily. He just shook his head in response. The general was also wearing a parachute just like the president's. "You see this ring right here? Once you clear the ramp, just count to three and pull it hard. If nothing happens, then pull the reserve chute."

Roger wanted to ask the general what he meant by "if nothing happens" but he was pushed forward by the secret service agent toward the ramp. "Just follow me, Mr. President. This is easy. Just like jumping off a plane." Agent Bareman smiled at his clumsy attempt at humor, and gave President Thornton a thumbs-up signal just before sprinting out the back door. A few seconds later he saw the chute open and billow as it dropped toward the mountains below.

Roger looked over at General Ashby. The general smiled. "Don't worry, Mr. President these things almost always work." And then he pushed the President of the United States out of the plane.

Roger clung desperately to the metal ring of the parachute as the wind hit him and whipped him around. The cold wind hit his face, making his eyes freeze so he could barely see. He looked up expecting to see the dome of a big parachute billowing above him, but was disappointed to see nothing but empty air. It was at that moment that he knew he was going to die, his body smashed and broken beyond recognition against the granite rocks of the Rocky Mountains.

And then he saw General Ashby's parachute floating above and to his right. He looked down and saw the mountain peaks rushing up around him, getting closer with each second. A million thoughts rushed through his mind as he prepared for his imminent death. He would be with his wife soon in heaven. He'd never liked air travel. He hadn't finished his coffee. And then he remembered the metal ring in his hand. He pulled it and the chute rose above him and billowed out. There was a heavy jerk as he began to slow his descent.

The president looked up and saw General Ashby high above him, blowing to the west, getting smaller and smaller until he was just a tiny dot in the sky. The C-130 was no longer visible, and he wondered if it had already crashed. Then he noticed several other parachutes closer to the general, but they seemed very far away ... too far away, and he wondered ... how will they find me? Roger looked down and saw the mountain range below him; the trees were quickly gaining in size as he watched help-lessly inside the parachute harness. He watched in awe for several seconds as the trees got closer and closer. And then it occurred to him. *I don't know how to land.*

His legs hit the tallest branches in the pine tree first, spinning him end over end as he crashed down through the boughs of the tree. He felt his legs snag on one tree limb after another, slowing his descent, then felt a vicious tug on his leg as he heard the sickening snap of breaking bone. Then he hit his head and everything went black.

Pigeon Creek, Idaho

SAMANTHA HAD CALMED DOWN NOW AFTER AN hour on the road. She looked up ahead and saw the Pigeon Creek sign and smiled. Matt had fallen asleep a few min-utes ago, and she didn't want to wake him. She continued on through the tiny town and drove past Alexandra and Marvin's new bugout home. She glanced over in the dark-ness, but couldn't see a whole lot. She just hoped they had finished building it in time.

And then Matt's driveway came into view on the right. The headlights of the truck lit it up. Suddenly she slammed on the brakes as a coyote rushed out in front of them. Matt's head jolted forward but was kept under control by the shoulder harness. His eyes popped open and he was immediately awake.

"What was that?"

Sam reached over and patted his left shoulder. "Sorry, honey. It was just some kind of animal, a big dog or something. I had to stop really fast."

Matt looked around at his surroundings and smiled. "Sam, we made it! You got us back okay!"

Sam thought it odd that she was happy about his praise, that she would be proud of a simple thing like driving a truck for an hour. But then she thought, *but this is special. Now I'm driving in the apocalypse.* It was funny, because the drive back home had been so anti-climactic, so quiet, so peaceful. Once they'd turned off the radio and Matt had fallen asleep, it was as if none of the bombs had fallen, as if none of the destruction and death had even occurred. There had been nothing but an eerie sort of quiet and peace as she drove the mountain roads.

She pulled into the driveway and drove up to the cabin. She slammed on the brakes again. There, in the middle of the dirt drive was a very large, dead black bear, and it was surrounded by five hungry timber wolves; they were growling as they sank their huge teeth into the bear's hide and ripped out large chunks of meat which they devoured quickly. Samantha looked over at Matt with fear in her eyes. "Matt, is this normal?"

For the first time since the apocalypse, Matt smiled. Then he laughed out loud. "It's okay, Sam. I'll just fire a couple of shots and scare them off."

And then she remembered. "You don't have your gun, Matt. We put it back inside the cabin before they took you to the hospital. It's still inside."

Matt let out a frustrated sigh, and then he reached over with his left hand and honked the horn several times. The wolves looked up but didn't leave. Two of them bared their teeth and snarled at the invasive truck. He honked the horn again with no better results. Finally he leaned back in the truck seat and sighed.

"I guess we wait here in the truck until they're finished eating. Then they'll go back to their den and we can go inside."

"But Matt. Can't you make them go away?"

Matt looked over at her, his eyes smiling. He painfully leaned over onto the console and rested his elbow there so he could be closer to her.

"It's okay, honey. They'll leave when their bellies are full. I don't usually have a pack of wolves on my front door step. It's nothing to worry about." And then he smiled. "I guess it gives new meaning to the phrase 'The wolves are at the door.'"

Samantha didn't know what to say to that, so she held her tongue. The city-girl part of her wanted to yell and scream and cry, but she exercised restraint. Matt had already saved her life twice, so she had no rational reason to doubt his abilities now.

"You must be pretty sore right now. You going to be okay?"

Matt nodded to her, then he reached over and pressed the ignition button to turn off the engine. "I'll be okay. No sense in wasting gas though. I have a feeling it's going to get pretty hard to find in a day or two."

A few seconds later the headlights turned off, and they were left in darkness. Sam could still see the shadow of the bear carcass in front of the truck, with several shadows milling around the drive, but it was almost like the wolves were a million miles away now.

"Everything's going crazy, Matt. What's going to happen now?"

Matt mistakenly thought she wanted to know the likely sequence of events that would take place over the next few days, so he explained it to her.

"It depends. If the attacks decline, and only several major American cities were struck, then we'll be okay here. It won't be the same as normal, but ..." And he struggled silently to explain it to her without scaring her. In the end, he just blurted it out. "Most people have only a few days of food in their pantries. The resupply trucks won't be running anymore. Whatever the stores have now is all that's available. Tomorrow there will be a huge run on the banks. People will take out all their money. Then they will go to the stores and buy everything on the shelves. Once people realize no more food is coming, they'll panic. Some will wait for the government to rescue them. Others will take matters into their own hands and begin looting, rioting, even killing their neighbors. The cities won't be a safe place."

And then he looked over at her and smiled again. "But we have plenty of food. We're hundreds of miles away from any big cities. We should be okay."

Just then one of the larger wolves jumped up onto the hood of the truck. He settled down peacefully, soaking up the heat from the engine block. He looked directly into the windshield but couldn't see past the glass inside.

Samantha looked over at Matt. She was trying to be brave, but not quite making it. "Are we going to end up as Purina Wolf Chow?"

He gently tried to reassure her. "It's going to be okay.

I've been preparing for this for years. The wolves can't get inside, so we'll just wait here until they leave." He reached up onto the dash shelf and picked up his cell phone. "Go ahead and check your cell to see if there are any messages from Alex and Marv."

They both awakened their cell phones, but no messages were waiting. Matt went into his news app and read off some of the headlines to her.

"Check this out. *Tokyo Hit by Three Nuclear Weapons*."

He paused. "Listen to this. *Pakistan and India Unleash Fire from the Sky*."

Samantha had her news app open now, and she began reading off headlines as well. *"Russian Advance on Poland Stalled by Tactical Nukes.* And then she looked over at Matt. "What's a tactical nuke?"

Matt answered her as he continued to scroll through the headlines. "It's just a smaller nuclear device that can be deployed on the battle field. I imagine we used a bunch of them to stop the Russians from taking over Europe."

Sam nodded. "It says here the Russians nuked China."

Matt scrolled down some more. "Yeah, and here it says China nuked Russia. I don't think there's going to be a whole lot of winners in this war."

And then Matt looked out the truck window into the darkness and frowned. "We need to be taking some Potassium Iodide first thing in the morning."

Samantha looked over at him quizzically. He saw her confused look and forced a smile onto his face. "It's nothing to worry about, honey. The fallout from Seattle should blow north of us, but we should take some Potassium Iodide just to be safe. It saturates your thyroid so it can't absorb radiation."

Sam looked out the window at the feeding wolves.

This was crazy. She was in the mountains. Her home was nuclear ash, and just a few feet away wolves were tearing away at a dead bear, and she was calling a man honey, that she'd known only a few weeks.

"So, are we going to die from radiation poisoning then?"

Matt shrugged and looked over at her sympathetically. "Probably not. We should get very little radiation in this part of the country, but back east. It could get really bad. The prevailing winds blow from west to east, so they'll get a lot more exposure than we will. We should stay inside for a few days though just to be safe."

Suddenly, Samantha wanted to be held. She unbuckled her seat belt and flipped up the console so she could sit on his lap. She wrapped her arms around him and held on tight. She wasn't heavy, but Matt's shoulder wreaked of pain as she clung to him. He forced himself to stay silent as the pain overwhelmed him.

And then Matt did the only thing that made sense. He opened his mouth and prayed.

"Dear God. Every day is a gift from you. Please be with all the people of the world. Many are suffering and dying right now. But we are safe, and we thank you for this cabin and this mountain where we are surrounded by friends." One of the wolves growled and snapped at another. Then it grew quiet again. "Thank you for the breath of life. Please be with Alex and Marv. Get them safely back home to us unharmed. We know that you love us, that you care about us, and that you will always be with us, even until the end of the age. God you are good. Help us to be faithful."

Matt pressed the lever on the side of his seat and leaned it back to the reclining position. He grimaced in pain, then swallowed it in silence. He moved back and Samantha lay on top of him. He could feel her wet tears against his cheek. He knew she wasn't ready for this. But then again, who was?

After several minutes, Matt felt her slow and steady breathing and knew she was asleep. Matt smiled and thanked God for sending him a companion. At least now he wouldn't have to face the apocalypse alone.

He thought it strange that he felt so calm and at peace as the world reeled and civilization burned around him. But here, up here, in the peace and solitude of the Rocky Mountains, it all seemed to make sense. He was here. Samantha was here. And, most important ... God was here with them.

As he watched the shadows of the wolves feeding on the dead bear, Matt smiled and squeezed Samantha firmly. It would be okay. It would be all right. God was with them, and he was reminded of a verse in the Bible. *Never will I leave you. Never will I forsake you.*

Ten minutes later Matt was sleeping as well.

24 Then the Lord rained down burning sulfur on Sodom and Gomorrah—from the Lord out of the heavens. 25 Thus he overthrew those cities and the entire plain, destroying all those living in the cities—and also the vegetation in the land.

Genesis 19:24-25 (NIV)

CHAPTER 2

Yakima, Washington

MARVIN LOOKED OUT AT THE city of Yakima as it lay nestled in the valley below. It seemed beautiful and peaceful as the residents were either still sleeping or inside their homes watching the horrific news on television. The full reality of America's plight had not yet begun to sink in.

Yakima was a city of about 100,000 people, but, on a normal day, it was pleasant in its feel, and much too naive to survive the apocalypse. Nonetheless, once people realized the full extent of the situation, then all hell would break loose. Even if cooler, more civilized heads were to prevail, eventually, people fleeing Seattle would overrun the city and devour its goods like a giant cloud of black locusts, rushing over the land. They were just too darn close to Seattle to be secure for long.

But, for now, Alex and Marv were still safe here. He was standing outside the Land Rover now, glaring down at the driver's side, back tire. It was as flat as a Kansas wheat field.

"I can't get anyone from the motor club on the phone, honey. All I get is a busy signal."

Alexandra stepped out of the Land Rover and onto the pavement. Marvin had pulled off to the side of the road where there was a wide shoulder and a level spot for jacking up the vehicle.

Marvin looked over at her and smiled. He'd known she wouldn't be able to get any help on the phone. Things were changed now, but his beautiful wife was going to have problems adapting to the new world. He recalled last night, even after Washington DC had been nuked, she'd still hesitated at the door and asked him if he thought it was cool enough to wear the sports outfit she had on. Of course, he'd said yes without even looking.

It was about 8AM and the sun was starting to warm up the air. "What are we going to do, honey?"

Marv looked over at her and laughed. "Just because I'm filthy rich, doesn't mean I don't know how to change a flat tire." He took one more look at the deflated tire, then moved around to get out the spare tire and the jack.

Alex hovered over him as he worked. "Are you sure you can do this, Marvin? I've never seen you do this before."

Marv smiled discreetly. "I wasn't always rich, honey. It's been a while but I think I can still do it." And then he looked up at her and winked. Alex smiled back at him as he placed the jack under the car.

"I'm so lucky to have you, Marv."

He picked up the lug wrench. "That's true, Alex. You

are." She reached down and slapped him playfully on top of the head. Marv ignored her and then he unlocked the lug nuts and began to loosen them one by one.

A few minutes later the tire was off and he rolled the spare into place. Alex looked up and then down the road. "Do you hear that, sweetheart? It sounds like a car. Maybe they can help."

A look of concern came over Marv as he glanced in the direction of the noise. "We don't need any help. I'll be done here in a few minutes. Then we can be on our way."

The car came into view. It was going at a high rate of speed, so Marvin gently pulled Alex off the road and further onto the shoulder so she didn't get hit. It looked like the car was going to drive on by, but at the last minute the driver locked up the brakes and skidded to a stop about 20 feet beyond them. It was then that Marv heard the loud music. The car backed up and the driver's power window came down, letting smoke and noise billow out into the otherwise pristine setting.

Eastern Idaho

Joshua Gimble looked up at the parachutes falling out of the C-130 and pursed his lips together. He shook his head in disgust. The plane was going to crash, and then the mountain would be filled with rescuers looking for survivors. It happened every year, some hiker would get lost, or get eaten by a bear and then his peace and quiet would be gone for days, sometimes weeks at a time. And then he thought to himself, _why can't people get eaten someplace else?_

And then he saw the man falling almost directly above him. Still a tiny speck, the man came closer and closer, all the while growing larger and larger, and Joshua thought to himself. *That man's not very good at this whole parachuting thing is he.* And then, suddenly, as Joshua watched, the parachute came open and the man was tossed about like a rag doll beneath the white canopy. Joshua was on the side of the valley where it began sloping upward, covered with pines. The parachute drifted closer.

Josh thought to himself, *If that man dies, then they'll be an investigation and I'll never get any peace and quiet.* He decided to help the man out, so he took off hiking up the slope toward the projected landing zone.

Josh heard the man's body crashing through the tree limbs while still a hundred yards away. He spoke out loud to himself. "Oh, that's just great! Go ahead and hurt yourself and make it even harder on me."

He walked over to the tree and saw the man hanging upside down by the parachute cords with his head only about three feet off the ground. He reached to the sheath at his belt and pulled out the Kershaw skinning knife and slashed the chute cords. The man's head and shoulders fell to the ground with a thud.

Reaching down with his other hand, he checked for a pulse on the man's throat. "Great. Still alive." Josh sat down beside the man's body and put his knife back in the sheath. He thought it odd that this parachutist was wearing a tailored Italian suit. He stuck his right hand into his left breast pocket and pulled out some deer jerky. It was honey sweet barbecue; one of his favorite flavors. He bit some off and put the rest back in his dirty pocket.

He reached down and pushed the man's cheek off to one side as he studied him. "You sure are one strange SOB aren't ya." He stared as he finished chewing the jerky. Then he saw the goose foot plant growing up through the dirt beside him. That was unusual this late in the year. He lowered his hand and plucked up the plant roots and all, shoved the top into his mouth and stripped off the leaves with his teeth and began to chew. "Hmm, still mild."

Goose foot grew all over North America and was quite edible, tasting a lot like spinach if you got it young enough. Some people called it Lambsquarters. Josh spit a tiny bit of pine needle out of his mouth and looked back down at the man. He was moving now.

Josh pulled a water bottle out of his side pocket of his jacket, unscrewed the top and poured a heathy splash into the man's face. The man stirred even more, so Josh slapped him on the right cheek several times until his eyes fluttered open.

Just to be safe, Josh reached over to his shoulder holster and drew the 44 magnum revolver and held it out in front of him. *No sense in taking any chances with a stranger*. When the man spoke his voice was weak and shaky.

"Are you going to put me out of my misery?"

Josh smiled and reholstered his pistol. Finally, he spoke to the man.

"Nah. Don't think so. Least wise not today." And then he looked over at the man's twisted left ankle and then at the blood flowing down his forehead. "Looks like yer in a world a hurt mister." And then he paused. "You want some help?"

The President of the United States looked up at the man and grimaced. The throbbing in his head was only surpassed by the pain in his ankle.

"Yes, please. I would like some help."

Josh nodded, pleased with the man's polite manner. "Thought so." And then he reached down and pulled out his knife again. "I'm gonna cut through yer pant leg so's I kin get a good look at that leg. I think it's busted fer sure." Josh cut the cloth and probed the ankle with his hands. Roger screamed as loud as he could.

"Hmm, I'm guessin' that hurts." He looked back at Roger's face. "Am I right?"

Roger stopped screaming as soon as Josh stopped touching the injury. "Yes, sir. It hurts most abundantly."

Josh reared his head back and laughed almost as loud as Roger had screamed. "That's a funny one. Abundantly. I tell ya. Abundantly. I don't think I've heard a soul talk like that in a coon's age."

The pain was so intense that Roger's eyesight was starting to blur over. He took a deep breath and tried to talk in full sentences. "My protection detail." He paused long enough to suck in a deep breath. "Where are they?"

Josh cocked his head to one side and smiled. "Protection detail?" And then he shook his head back and forth as if disappointed. "Young man. You ain't got no protection detail, ceptin' me." He paused and looked up into the sky. The plane and the other parachutes were miles away by now.

"Listen, kid. I'll go ahead 'n splint the break and then drag ya down the mountain, but after that yer on yer own. Got it?"

Roger nodded. "Thanks. It's okay. I'm the President of the United States. You'll be well compensated for your troubles."

Josh smiled and nodded. "Yep. That's right yer the president and I'm Howdy Doody." He reached back into his jacket pocket and bit off another piece of jerky. "You must a hit yer head pretty hard there, boy." He extended his dirty hand out to Roger. "You want some jerky?"

Roger started to shake his head and immediately regretted it. The motion made him vomit out onto the brown pine needles and onto the man's black, leather boot. The man looked at it and frowned.

"That's not very hospitable."

Roger wanted to answer him, but he couldn't. The pain was just too great. The man seemed to sense this and nodded his head a bit.

"Okey dokey there, buddy. Here's what I'm gonna do." He paused long enough to take another bite of jerky, but this time instead of chewing, he shoved it with his tongue into the left side of his cheek for later. "I'm gonna go ahead and splint this leg. Then I'm gonna make a litter 'n drag yer sorry butt down the slope to my cabin. Then I'll call fer help 'n you kin get outta here."

Josh smiled. "Sound like a plan?"

Roger tried to nod, but wasn't sure if he'd succeeded. Since it was a rhetorical question, it didn't matter. Josh stood up and went off in search of good sticks to make a splint. While he was away, Roger thought about his predicament. He was totally at the mercy of this mountain man whom he surmised was not entirely sane. He didn't know where the secret service was or General Ashby for that matter. He suspected they were miles away by now. But they would undoubtedly mount a rescue operation, so he just needed to stay alive for a while longer until they found him.

Five minutes later Josh returned with two sticks of the right thickness, strength and size. He lay them on the pine needled ground and then reached into his right, lower jacket pocket. He pulled out a clear, glass bottle, unscrewed the cap and raised the opening to Roger's lips.

"Ya need to drink as much a this as ya can. It'll dull the pain."

But the president waved him off. "No, I never partake. I'm not a drinker."

"Josh nodded and raised the bottle to his own lips. "Well, okay then. I'll just half'ta drink enough fer both of us then."

Roger watched as the old man lifted the bottle and drained all the contents. When he was done he threw the bottle off to the side. Roger found himself thinking the craziest thoughts. *My leg is busted. My head is dented in. The world is in the process of nuclear annihilation, and I'm upset about one old man littering in the forest. I must be going crazy.*

"I got a feelin' yer gonna regret yer temprance, but hey. Ta each his own." And then he smiled showing his chipped and yellow-stained teeth. "A man's gotta do, what a man's gotta do."

Josh placed each stick to either side of the broken ankle. Then he took off his boot laces. He laughed out loud. "Last chance Mr. President. I kin still put ya outta yer misery if'n ya like."

It was odd, but Roger actually hesitated at the man's offer. He gave it consideration, but then quickly refused. "No thanks. I'll take my chances."

And Josh slid the boot laces underneath the broken ankle and situated them properly. Just before he reefed on the laces to tighten them down, Roger yelled for him to stop.

"Wait!"

Josh looked down at him. "What?" Then he nodded his head knowingly as he pulled the 44 magnum from his shoulder rig. "Ya changed yer mind, uh?" He lifted the barrel of the pistol up against the president's head and placed his finger on the trigger, but Roger yelled loud enough to make his head split wide open.

"No! Don't shoot! That's not what I meant."

Josh looked at him quizzically. "Ya don't want me ta put ya outta yer misery?"

"I just want to know your name, that's all."

Josh laughed out loud again, this time throwing back his head, exposing his hairy throat. Roger watched the man's adam's apple bob up and down while waiting. Finally the old man looked back down at him, his laugh suddenly reduced to a soft smile.

"Name's Josh. Joshua Gimble." And then he added as an after thought. "But all my friends just call me Weed." And then he drew both his hands together and the laces tightened the sticks up against the broken ankle. Searing pain shot up Roger's leg and into his brain. And, finally, when he could no longer take it ... he passed out.

Weed looked down as he was tying off the splint. "Don't say I didn't warn ya. Ya should'a drank the whisky."

And then he smiled again and laughed out loud as he talked. "President! He's the president! That's a good one. A real good one."

4 Before they had gone to bed, all the men from every part of the city of Sodom—both young and old—surrounded the house. 5 They called to Lot, "Where are the men who came to you tonight? Bring them out to us so that we can have sex with them.

Genesis 19:4-5 (NIV)

CHAPTER 3

<u>Yakima, Washington</u>

"**H**EY BOYS. LOOKY HERE. WE got us a damsel in distress!"

Marvin instinctively reached his right hand over to his wife and shielded her protectively. The driver got out of the car and stood defiantly beside it. Both doors on the other side opened as well, and two more men exited the vehicle. They were rough-looking men, unshaven with greasy hair in dire need of a comb. Marvin took a step closer to the Land Rover, pulling Alex along with him. He pasted a smile onto his face but said nothing as the three men took up position about halfway between their car and the Land Rover. Finally, Marvin spoke.

"That's close enough boys."

The leader hesitated about 20 feet away, and the other two men stopped behind him. The leader's wide mouth grinned. He held out his hands to both sides of his body in an effort to appear nonthreatening.

"Relax, man. We just wanna help. We saw the young lady here and thought she might need some help changin' the tire." He brought his arms back in and brushed his flannel shirt back to reveal a 357 magnum revolver tucked inside his waist band. "You got a problem with that?"

Marvin saw it, but didn't let his eyes rest upon it. He just smiled back, trying to look as confident as possible under the situation.

"That won't be necessary boys. I appreciate the sentiment, but I've got things well in hand here." Marvin guided Alex so she was completely concealed by the Land Rover. Then he took up his own position behind the engine block. And then Marvin felt the most unusual calm come over him. Everything slowed down around him. It was as if his senses had suddenly become fine tuned. He could hear a bird singing off about 20 yards behind him. The sun was glinting off the windshield of the other vehicle. A feeling of mild electricity ran down both Marv's shoulders, into his biceps, then his forearms and didn't stop until reaching his finger tips. Every muscle in his body felt taut and coiled.

Terror gripped Alex as she cowered down behind the Land Rover. Her whole body began to shake uncontrollably. She began to whimper softly, unable to keep her fear in check. The leader's right hand started to move a bit closer to the gun. Marvin yelled at the man as loud as he could.

"Don't do it, son!"

The man's hand suddenly hesitated. His face grew stern. Marvin crouched down just a bit lower behind the hood of the Land Rover, his own right hand tingling with anticipation. Marvin watched as the stranger reached over and began to draw his pistol from his waist. He reached down and cleared his own shirt from the one o'clock position and began to draw his Glock Model 19. Marvin drove the gun out in front of him in a two-handed grip and struggled to find the sights. He heard the mighty roar of the 357 magnum revolver and saw tiny bits and pieces of his Land Rover fly up in front of him. The man got off two shots before Marvin found his sights. He placed the front sight on the man's chest and pressed the trigger three times in rapid succession.

The stranger stopped shooting, and his gun began to lower. Marvin quickly moved his pistol sight to the man on the right, but he was already moving back behind their car. Marvin transitioned to the man on the left, but he was already moving as well. Alex peeked up over the Land Rover just in time to watch the leader of the group collapse slowly to the pavement. Then she watched as both men hopped into the car, fired up the engine and sped away, leaving their friend to bleed out on the road.

Marvin raised himself up slowly away from the hood of the vehicle. Then he moved his front sight back down to the man dying on the pavement. The sound of the fleeing car faded into the morning light. He looked over at his wife.

"Are you okay, Alex?"

She nodded and then screamed as loud as she could.

"Marvin! Honey! You're bleeding!"

Matt's Cabin

WHEN MATT FINALLY WOKE UP THE NEXT MORNing, sunlight was filtering down through the boughs of the

23

pine tree beside his house. What was left of the bear was still on the ground in front of the truck, but the wolves were gone now. And then he felt Samantha move atop his chest and heard her steady breathing. He tried to shift his legs, but he was totally numb from the waist down. Matt's eyes moved to rest on her face, which was only a few inches away from his eyes. She looked so peaceful that he didn't want to awaken her. But he knew that he should; they had so many things they needed to do.

Despite the sense of urgency, he just looked at her a few minutes, watching her long eye lashes, smelling the beautiful yellow-blonde hair that was resting lightly against his face. He took in her smell as he relished the rising and falling of her body as she breathed lightly against his chest. Finally, he spoke softly.

"Honey, we need to wake up now."

Sam stirred softly but her eyes didn't open.

"Samantha, dear, we need to wake up. The wolves are gone."

Her beautiful eyes fluttered open, then closed, then opened again. She raised her head up off his shoulder and smiled.

"Hi."

Matt smiled.

"Hello."

Then she turned on his lap and saw the dead bear on the driveway and the cabin just beyond it.

"The wolves are gone, Matt."

He nodded his head. "I told you they would leave. And, as you know, I'm always right."

Samantha turned her head back to Matt and laughed softly. "Oh really?"

Matt nodded. "That's right."

She kissed his forehead lightly. "Well, you were certainly right when you decided to fall in love with me."

Matt thought that statement was a bit odd, and so he pondered it before answering her. He'd known her for just a few weeks. How could he be in love with her? His lips moved into a gentle smile. He listened to his heart, and it told him the truth.

"Yes, I am in love with you."

Sam moved her face out to get a better look at him. "Of course you are. You are hopelessly, madly, irretrievably in love with me!"

The feeling was starting to come back into his legs now. Then the tingling overwhelmed him as the blood reached his feet and he started to laugh without restraint.

Samantha frowned. "Why is that so funny?"

Matt started to bounce up and down off the seat, and the more he moved, the more he laughed.

"What's so funny Matt!"

With a great deal of effort, Matt lifted his left leg off the truck floor and bounced it up and down several times, but that only made him laugh harder.

Now Samantha's face contorted into a frown. "Don't you dare laugh at me when I say you love me!"

Matt bounced his right leg and laughed again. Sam moved away from him and then hopped back over into the driver's seat. Finally, the tingling in his legs began to subside, and he was able to stop laughing and talk to her.

"I'm ... sorry, Samantha." His breathing leveled off as he regained his composure. "You slept on my lap all night and my legs were asleep. They were tickling like crazy."

The look on Samantha's face softened again. Matt reached his left hand over and caressed her cheek. "Of course I love you, Sam. How could I not love you."

Sam smiled again. "Okay then. Glad we got that out of the way. I love you too." And then she looked at the half-eaten bear carcass in the driveway.

"Is it still the end of the world, Matt?"

Matt's face softened and he leaned across the seat to kiss her gently on the cheek. "Yes, dear. I'm afraid so. Things will never be the same again. People are dying everywhere. The apocalypse will be a very hard life."

Sam's silver-blue eyes saddened. "But at least we won't have to go through it alone. We have each other."

She leaned back over and kissed Matt full on the lips. He returned her kiss, but then quickly pulled away.

"Alex and Marvin!"

They both found their cell phones and pulled up their messages. Matt quickly deleted all the business messages since his business was no longer functional. Then he opened a few links and skimmed some news articles.

"Looks like the bombs have stopped falling, or at least slowed down. I got nothing from Marvin or Alex though."

Sam's face was stern as she read. "Listen to this from Alex."

We made it out of Seattle. Near Yakima. Marv just killed a man. He got shot. Will text more later.

Samantha raised her head up; there was a look of shock and amazement on her face. "Marv killed a man. He's shot?"

The news shocked them both back into the harsh reality of the apocalypse. Matt put down his cell phone and stared straight ahead. He was forming a list of things he needed to do right away before the final vestiges of civility fell apart. Samantha rested her head down onto the steering wheel and began to cry softly. Matt reached over and caressed her back in circular motions.

"It's okay, Sam. They're alive. We know that now. And they made it out of Seattle."

He paused, waiting for her response, but none came save the quiet sobbing. He watched as tears fell from her face and down onto the black, rubber floor mat beneath her. He felt sorry for her, but he didn't know what else to do. He'd been preparing for this for years, but this was still all quite new to Samantha.

Finally, a steely resolve came over him, and he knew exactly what to do.

"Text her back, Sam. Ask if they need us to come to them. Tell her to enable tracking on her cell phone so we have their real-time position. That way if they get in trouble we at least have a starting point to look for them."

Matt took one last look outside the truck, just to make sure there were no wolves about. Then he opened his door and walked around the front and opened Sam's door. He leaned inside the cab and gave her a hug before gently helping her out onto the sandy driveway. The air was heavy with the scent of bear carcass.

"Let's go inside and get cleaned up. Then I'll cook breakfast and we can figure out what to do."

Samantha nodded and leaned heavily on Matt's wounded shoulder as he helped her into the cabin.

Just outside Yakima

ALEXANDRA LOWERED HER CELL PHONE AND LOOKED over at her husband. "Marvin. What are we going to do? You just killed a man."

The strange calm that Marv had felt during the gun fight was ebbing away now, like an unnatural tide he'd never felt before. He looked down at the dead body on the pavement. Blood seeped out and touched the soles of his shoes. He moved back a pace to keep them clean. Marv reached down and picked the revolver up off the road. It was clean of blood, so he shoved it into the small of his back.

Alexandra finally regained her composure and moved over closer to her husband. Her shaky hands unbuttoned his shirt and pulled it off him to reveal the wound near the top of his left shoulder. Blood was seeping out onto his back and chest, but the clotting had already started.

"It's just a flesh wound. We'll wrap it up, put some pressure on it and it'll be fine."

"Marvin, what are you doing with that gun? You can't take that! It's evidence."

But Marvin ignored her. Instead, he reached down and grabbed the dead man's arm and began to drag him off the road and into the ditch. Alexandra's mouth fell open in astonishment.

"What are you doing, Marvin!"

But Marvin ignored her again. He gave the body a push with the sole of his boot and sent it rolling into the tall grass at the side of the road.

"Marvin, you're going to get in trouble for this. Those two are probably already talking to the police. The cops will be here any minute now and they'll arrest you. We need to call the police right away, Marv!"

Marv stopped and looked up and over at his wife.

"Really, honey. That's what we need to do? Call the police?"

He walked back over to the car and inspected the damage to the hood of the Land Rover.

"Reach in there and pop the hood for me, babe."

Alex was still in a semi-state of shock so she was slow

in complying. Marv lifted the hood and looked for damage inside the engine compartment. He saw none, so he dropped the hood back down with a slam. Then he looked at the pavement underneath the Land Rover to check for fluid leaks.

"We got lucky, Alex. No damage."

Marv moved to the back of the vehicle and continued changing the tire. He talked to her as he did so.

"Please listen for vehicles. If you hear one please get my attention." He sat his butt down on the pavement and slid the wheel onto the hub. "We won't be calling the police anymore, honey. Our phones aren't working and we can't text them. And even if we could I wouldn't do it. That would just slow us down." He paused and looked over at her. "We're in transition between civilization and total anarchy. It's quite possible that I might have to kill more people before this is done." He screwed on the first nut with his bare hands. "What we need to do right now is get to the cabin. If we don't do that, then we'll die. That's the bottom line."

He screwed on the second nut. "From now on we handle things on our own. We can't count on the police anymore."

He finished screwing on the nuts, then tightened them in a cross-bolt pattern with the tire iron. The whole time he was working, Alex just stared over at the place where her husband had rolled the body into the tall grass. Then she looked down and watched the blood congeal on his back.

She lifted the phone and tried to call Samantha, but all she got was a busy signal. Alex leaned her body up against the side of the Land Rover and began to cry.

> *"God has blessed you richly, so get down on your knees and thank him. Don't forget the less fortunate or God will personally kick your ass. I'd love to do it for him, but I can't be everywhere."*
>
> *– Willie Nelson*

CHAPTER 4

On the Road Again

"T HE LIFE I LOVE IS MAKIN' MUSIC WITH my friends, cuz I can't wait to get on the road again!"

Alexandra covered her ears in a vain attempt to block out her husband's screeching impersonation of Willie Nelson. "Stop it, Marvin! Just shut up with the Willie Nelson, please, before I go crazy!"

Marvin stopped singing and looked over at his wife. He raised one eyebrow just slightly before responding to her. "I'm sorry, honey. I thought you liked Willie Nelson."

Alex turned away from him and looked out the window of the Land Rover as the landscape passed them by. Yakima was behind them now, and she wasn't exactly sure where they were.

"Of course I like Willie." She paused and pursed her lips before continuing. "I just don't like it when you try to sound like him."

Marvin grit is teeth in exasperation. She'd been like this

ever since the flat tire incident. "I love ya honey, but I don't know what's got your undies all up in a bunch."

Something inside Alex snapped as she turned back to face her husband. She began slapping him on the side of the head as she yelled. "You just killed a man! You shot him. And then you dragged him off the road and left him for the vultures!"

As best he could while being slapped, Marvin veered off onto the shoulder of the road as he slowed the car to a stop. Blood was seeping down the right side of his face. It paused at the base of his chin before dropping down onto his jeans. When it was safe to take his hands off the steering wheel, he grabbed onto his wife's flailing hands and clamped down tightly. She struggled to get loose, but Marvin held down even tighter.

"Alex!" She said nothing. "Alex! Look at me!" But she looked straight down into her lap. "Look at me, Alex." Marvin lowered the tone of his voice. She stopped struggling, and Marvin loosened his grip. She was crying now, the sobs making her chest heave up and down in grief.

"It's okay, baby." He reached over and stroked the left side of her cheek with the back of his right hand. When he spoke, it was softly, like the whispering of the wind. "I'm the same man you married, Alex. I haven't changed. I still love you."

A few cars sped past them, but Marvin paid no attention to them. He'd turned off I-82 onto WA-221 to avoid the traffic, but more and more people were fleeing to the east, away from Seattle. He leaned over and hugged his wife. At first she didn't respond. Marvin kissed her head over and over again. "It's okay, Alex. I love you."

Finally, she reached back and returned his embrace. When she looked up, her eyes were red and puffy, and tears were streaming down her cheeks. Alex shook her head slowly back and forth. "I don't know what's wrong with me, Marvin." She sniffed before going on. "I ... I think I'm falling apart."

Marvin smiled softly. "That's okay, baby. I understand." But in his heart, he knew that was a lie. It wasn't okay, and he didn't understand why she'd just scratched his face. Nonetheless, he had to pretend for her sake. Because he loved her, and because it would do no good for both of them to fall apart. So Marvin pushed his emotions down, sealed them off to wait for another day.

"Talk to me, Alex."

It took her a few seconds to get control of her sobbing, but she finally looked up and over at her husband. But when she saw the blood on his face, she started to cry all over again. "Oh, Marv I'm so sorry. I didn't mean to hurt you. I don't know what's wrong with me."

Marvin held her tight and tried to calm her down. "It's okay, Alex. I'm okay. It's just a scratch."

"But I did it to you. I hurt you."

She reached down on the floor of the Land Rover and picked up her purse. Alex pulled out a small packet of wet wipes and began to softly dab away at the blood. Marvin let her finish cleaning him off before saying anything. When he did, it was slowly and carefully, as if each word had a force all its own.

"The world has changed, Alex."

Alex nodded her head.

"I know. My mom and dad are dead."

Marvin said nothing. Her parents had been visiting in Los Angeles, so she was probably right.

"My house is all burned up."

Her hands started to shake, so Marvin reached over and

grabbed onto them gently. They were ice cold. He squeezed just enough to reassure and warm her.

"I know, honey. But you and I aren't dead. Samantha and Matt aren't dead either. We have another house, and we're going there right now."

Marvin took a moment to raise his head and glance around him just to make sure they were safe. They seemed to be in the middle of nowhere, surrounded by open fields, but the shoot-out had left him rather nervous and on edge.

"Things have changed, and you and I have to change or we won't make it."

Through her quiet sobbing, Alex spoke, her shaky voice just barely audible. "But ... what if I don't want to live like this? What if I can't do it?"

Marvin smiled softly. "You can do it. You can and you will. I know you, Alex. You're not just another pretty face." He paused just long enough to brush her beautiful, brown hair away from her face. "You are stronger than you know. And together, you and I are going to discover that new strength." He paused again. "We have to, Alex. Because I can't do this alone." He stroked her right cheek again. "I need you, Alex. I need someone to love. And I need someone to protect."

Alex looked up and over at her husband. She continued to cry as she fell into his arms and wept.

"Oh, Marvin. I don't deserve you."

Her husband held her back and squeezed her firmly around the shoulders. "Don't think that for a minute, sweetheart. We deserve each other, and we're going to make it."

Husband and wife sat together in the car, holding one another, both giving and drawing strength from each other. Marvin kissed the top of her brunette head again.

"It doesn't matter what happens honey. The world can

fall apart, but you and I will hold together. It's you and me, babe. You and me against the world."

And, at that moment, Alexandra began to pull herself together. She found her inner strength, that part of her that wanted to live and fight and protect the man she loved. She snuggled her face into his chest. She could smell the blood on his shirt, both the dried blood from the gunshot and the fresh blood from his face. And she vowed to herself never to fall apart again.

"I love you, Marvin."

Marvin smiled.

"I love you too, Alex."

Marvin looked up and out past the hood of the Land Rover. That's when he saw the cloud of steam rising up around the grille of his car. He glanced down at the temperature gauge and confirmed that his car was overheating.

He sighed and shook his head. *Oh well, whoever said the apocalypse was going to be easy?*

Pigeon Creek

AFTER BOTH OF THEM HAD TAKEN A SHOWER AND PUT ON clean clothes, Matt made them a light breakfast of steel-cut oatmeal, apple juice and toast. Then Sam took the time to clean and rebandage his wounds. After that, Samantha stayed inside the cabin while Matt strapped on his Ruger five-seven. His chest felt like it had been pounded with a meat cleaver, so he took six ibuprofen to soften the pain. He kissed Samantha gently on the cheek.

"I'll leave this AR-15 right here propped up by the door in case the wolves come back." He quickly showed her how to use it again.

"Do you think they'll come back, Matt?"

Matt smiled. "No, of course not. If I thought they'd come back, then I wouldn't be leaving you alone here. I just need to get that dead bear out of my driveway. It already smells pretty ripe. You'll be perfectly safe. I'll just be about 15 minutes."

Samantha nodded and hugged him one last time before he headed out the door of the cabin. Matt winced in pain when she squeezed him.

From inside the cabin, Sam listened as Matt strapped the chain around the bear's leg and then hitched it to the back of the truck. The truck door slammed shut and the man she loved drove away, leaving her all alone.

For a few seconds, she listened as the sound of the truck engine faded into the distance, then she turned back to the picture window overlooking the kitchen. The cabin was small and rather spartan, but very cozy and she liked it. She looked out the window down the sloping mountainside and smiled. It was hard to believe, looking out at all this pristine beauty, that the world was burning and people were dying all over the country. She thought about it for a second. *No, not just the country ... but the entire planet.*

She thought about her mother and father. She knew that they were probably dead, and the thought wiped the gentle smile from her face. They were oblivious to politics and the state of the world and had always been so by choice. Samantha hoped in her heart that they'd died together and quickly.

And then she thought of Marvin and her sister. She pulled out her cell phone. She had no service, so she went outside to get out from under the steel roof of the cabin. Just for a few seconds she saw one bar and it quickly went away. There was a message from her sister.

Hey Sam. We are southeast of Yakima now.

We were attacked, but Marvin killed one and drove the others away. Will be heading down 82 through NE Oregon into Idaho. I'm not doing well. I need my baby sister to talk to. Text when you can. I love you.

Her feelings were ambivalent, swirling through her heart like a cyclone. Marvin had killed a man. But they were okay. Safe. But then again, how safe could they be if people were attacking them and Marvin had to kill people to get through?

Samantha looked at the pine tree in front of the cabin. She saw the pool of blood that had soaked into the sand of the driveway just a few yards away. Flies were buzzing around it now, and the mid-morning sun was starting to heat things up. She looked over at the used-up garden and then walked over to it. She saw some green leaves jutting up out of the ground on something like a stalk. Matt had called it kale. She seemed ashamed of her ignorance, but ... she'd never seen kale in the ground before, only in the grocery store and the restaurant. She'd never seen anything in the ground except for maybe corn and wheat and only then from far away while driving down the road.

She walked over and bent down to look at it closer. She reached out and stroked the kale leaves softly. Then she tore one off and placed it hesitantly into her mouth. It tasted stronger than the kale she ate in the restaurant. She chewed and swallowed.

Samantha stood back up and walked over to the pine tree. She reached up and grabbed a fistful of needles and looked at them. Then she brought them up to her nose and smelled. She liked the scent. It reminded her of the man she loved. Sam pulled the needles loose and walked past the bloody driveway and into the cabin.

Once inside, she grabbed the cast iron kettle off the wood stove and brought it over to the sink. She'd never seen a hand pump inside a house before. She placed the kettle beneath the spout and started to pump the handle up and down. Nothing happened. Finally, on the tenth pump water began to trickle out. She filled the kettle, dropped in the needles and placed the kettle back on the wood stove.

She looked around the cabin and sighed. There was so much she'd have to learn to do. Matt had called it living off the grid.

Just then she heard the sound of a vehicle pulling into the driveway. She ran outside to greet Matt, but was surprised to see a police SUV and a man stepping out. At first he looked surprised to see her, but then a look of recognition came over his face.

"Are you Samantha?"

Sam had a million thoughts running through her mind, so she just nodded.

"Well, my wife told me you were beautiful, and I can see she wasn't exaggerating." He paused. "So where's Matt?"

Sam took a small step back toward the cabin door. It was then the man realized he'd scared her. He smiled.

"It's okay, I'm Luke Gibbons." Sam still said nothing. "I'm Theresa's husband from down at the diner. I've known Matt for years. We go to church together."

Samantha finally smiled and took a step forward. Luke walked up to her slowly, extending his right hand.

"It's good to meet you, Samantha."

Sam accepted his hand and he grasped it lightly and shook it. Then he looked around the driveway, saw the wolf tracks and the blood drying into the ground.

"What's with all the blood?" And then he answered the question for her. "Ah, from the bear carcass. And some wolves came to feed on it I see?"

Sam nodded. "Yes, Matt is out getting rid of the body right now."

Just then the sound of Matt's truck grew from distant to near. In a few seconds he pulled up and got out of his truck. He was moving slowly and he winced as he held his right arm out to shake Luke's hand. The healing wounds on his chest were throbbing from the exertion.

"Good to see you, Luke."

The police officer smiled. "Good to see you, too, Matt. You don't look so good."

Matt tried to force a smile onto his face, but didn't quite succeed. "I've been better."

Luke pointed down at the bloody driveway. "Sorry about the bear. I was planning on coming up here today to clean things up for you before you got back from the hospital, but ... well, things have gotten busy here in the last 24 hours."

A look of concern came over Matt's face. "So, are Theresa and the baby okay?"

Luke nodded. "Yeah. We're all fine. Most of Pigeon Creek is okay. And that's why I came up to see you." He paused. "We're having a community meeting down at the fire barn, and I was hoping you'd come down and talk to the folks. You know, calm them down, tell them what to expect and how to prepare for what's coming."

Matt looked over briefly at Samantha. She nodded her head. He turned back to Luke.

"Of course, what time?"

"Noon."

Matt nodded. "We'll see you then."

The police officer got back into his SUV and drove away. Matt walked over to Samantha and put his arm around her. He leaned down and kissed the top of her head. She hugged him back.

> *"I cook with wine, sometimes I even add it to the food."*
>
> – *W.C. Fields*

CHAPTER 5

Idaho Mountainside

WEED KNELT IN FRONT OF THE cast iron wood stove and held his hands out to warm them. It wasn't time for winter yet, but, still, his old bones seemed to suck in the damp and cold like a mountain sponge. Weed had lived here for the past 10 years, but it still felt like he'd just moved here. He liked the mountains, more particularly, he liked his little part of the mountains.

He looked over at the stranger in his bed, and then reached up to stroke the grey stubble of his beard. He didn't like people, never had and probably never would. That was a strange thing because he'd worked for a major corporation for 30 years in customer service before retiring. And now ... he was living out his dream. Solitude. Life without the intrusion of other humans. He had his books, and he had his favorite movies, and that's all he ever needed or wanted. Anything more than that made him grouchy.

For 30 years Weed had scrimped and saved money, and slowly built up this little homestead, totally off the grid and isolated from modern society. He had solar panels on the roof, wood stove for heat, and he grew his own fruits and vegetables and killed his own meat. It was a perfect retirement for a man who despised human interaction.

It wasn't that Weed hated people in general, he just didn't like them, and wanted nothing more than to be away from the complexity that inevitably came with community and interpersonal relationships. In that regard, he was a selfish man. But he had no regrets.

He reached up and lifted the cast iron tea kettle from atop the wood stove and poured himself a cup of sumac tea. He preferred Staghorn Sumac, but that didn't grow around here, so he settled for Smooth Sumac. But, of course, Weed had about 20 different teas that he harvested from the mountains, and he liked them all. He'd never been much of a coffee drinker.

Weed took another glance at the man in his bed and moved a step back and sat down in his wooden rocking chair. He picked up the book beside him and opened it up to his marker.

> *Laura felt a warmth inside her. It was very small, but it was strong. It was steady, like a tiny light in the dark, and it burned very low but no winds could make it flicker because it would not give up.*

Weed closed his eyes and felt the warmth of the fire in front of him. Some people would think it odd that a man like him was reading a Laura Ingalls Wilder book, but he didn't much care what people thought. That's why his 30 years working in customer service had been an agony for him. The whole time he'd been working there he'd longed for the time when he could tell them all to go to ... And then he heard the stranger roll over in bed. He glanced over his shoulder and saw the man still sleeping. Weed had the injured man's leg propped up on several pillows to keep it elevated.

Weed sighed and looked back down at his book and continued reading.

Mountain Home Air Force Base

GENERAL ASHBY STOOD IN FRONT OF THE TABLE inside the conference room at Mountain Home Air Force Base in Southwestern Idaho. For the past 24 hours since being rescued, he'd been frustrated by the slow progress in finding President Thornton. As the Chairman of the Joint Chiefs, he was considered the highest ranking officer in the US armed forces. Although he was considered the direct military advisor to the president, answering only to the president, he was strictly forbidden by law from taking operational command of individual military units. As such he was thwarted temporarily by the base commander when he'd tried to organize a search and rescue operation for President Thornton. Finally, after the president's Chief of Staff and the secret service had assured the Air Force that Ashby really was now a 4-star general, the base commander had begrudgingly relented and began cooperating with the general.

"This is where the plane finally went down, and here's where the president bailed out." Ashby pointed at the map with his cursor. "It's just south of a little town called

Pigeon Creek." He gazed around the room at the myriad of high- and middle-ranking officers in the room. "I need you to work up a search-and-rescue plan and I need it done yesterday."

No one in the room moved. "The country is in chaos, and we have no person with constitutional authority until we find the president." He paused. "Any questions?"

There was silence for a moment, then a Lieutenant Colonel raised his hand. General Ashby's voice sounded exasperated when he responded. "For god's sake don't raise your hand, colonel. We're not in kindergarten anymore." He motioned with his hands. "Just spit it out!"

The colonel cleared his throat. "Well, sir, I was just wondering how we know the president is still alive. No one saw his chute open."

General Ashby wanted to pick the colonel up by his lapels and slap him, but he restrained himself. "It doesn't matter. If he's alive, then bring him back here to run the country." He looked down and then back up again. "And if he's dead, then, well, we'll burn that bridge when we come to it."

He looked around the room slowly, letting his eyes rest on each man individually for effect. "But here's the butt-ugly truth gentlemen. America needs this man if we're to survive. In the short time I've been Chairman, I can tell you that he's the man for the job. He's decisive and strong, and right now America needs a strong leader if we're going to emerge from the ashes of this excrement sandwich."

The young colonel nodded, and the others in the room smiled slightly.

"Okay, men. You have 2 hours to come up with a plan and begin implementation. No one leaves the room until it's done." And then the new 4-star general turned and strode quickly and confidently out of the room.

Idaho Mountainside

Rᴏɢᴇʀ Tʜᴏʀɴᴛᴏɴ's ᴇʏᴇs ғʟᴜᴛᴛᴇʀᴇᴅ ᴏᴘᴇɴ, ᴛʜᴇɴ closed, then quickly opened again. He could smell the wood smoke from the stove along with something else that he didn't recognize. He tried to raise up his head, but quickly dropped it back down onto the pillow when his head filled with throbbing pain.

"Still hurts don't it."

Roger's memory was starting to clear now. The plane had crashed. He'd jumped out and crashed into a tree. His leg was broken. Roger waited a few more seconds to let his head clear.

"How long have I been sleeping?"

Weed grunted softly. "Almost a full day."

Roger groaned involuntarily. He was disappointed. "Have you seen anyone looking for me?"

Weed laughed out loud. "Haven't seen any secret service agents if that's what you mean."

The president shrugged. That's exactly what he meant, but ... it sounded silly to say it out loud, knowing that this man had no idea who he was. Roger tried to smile. "Right about now I'd settle for the Schwann's ice cream man."

Weed smiled and turned his rocking chair to face him. "Now that there's funny." He thought for a moment before continuing on. "So, what's yer real name?"

Roger considered his question before responding. This man obviously had no idea what was going on in the world or in the country. He decided to try one last time to convince him that he really was the President of the

United States.

"My name is Roger Thornton."

The man in the rocking chair stopped rocking. He looked up at the pine ceiling and then back down at him.

"That name sounds familiar. I've heard that before. Where ya from?"

"Missouri. I'm the Speaker of the House."

Weed reached down and picked up his cup of tea. "The Missouri State House?"

Roger took a deep breath before going on. "No, sir. The U.S. House of Representatives."

Weed smiled again and took another sip of tea. "Two days ago you said you was the President of the United States. Now yer only the House Speaker. It's hard ta trust a man what keeps changin' his story all the time."

Roger let out an exasperated sigh. "You have no idea what's been going on the past week or so do you?"

The old man began rocking again beside the fire. "I got no need ta know. The outside world don't matter up here in the mountains. Leastwise not ta me."

Now it was Roger's turn to smile. "I think what's been going on will matter even to you, Weed." And then he explained everything to him. The terrorist attacks on the East Coast, the missile attacks on the West Coast, the bombs falling all over the globe. How he'd been sworn in as the President of the United States. But Roger could tell by the look on Weed's face that he didn't believe him.

Roger thought for a moment. Then an idea came to him. "Have you looked into my wallet yet?"

Weed looked offended. "Course not! It ain't none a my business, 'n I don't steal. Ain't that kind a guy."

Roger slowly moved his head back and forth to keep it from aching. "I know that, Weed. But if you look inside my wallet, you'll see that I have a security pass that gets me in and out of the United States Capitol building. That will corroborate at least part of my story."

The old mountain man thought about that for a moment, then he calmly stood up from the chair and walked over to Roger's bedside. He slowly opened up the wallet he'd put on the stand beside the bed and quickly leafed through it. He stopped when he came to the ID card. It looked formal, with the official seal of Congress on it. He lifted it up to the light and gazed at it.

"Well I'll be ..." And then he put it back inside the wallet. "I ain't never seen one a those before."

And then he smiled. "So I kin take this here card and walk right into the Capitol 'n no body's gonna stop me?"

Roger started to say yes but then quickly stopped himself. "Well, no. Not anymore. Washington DC is radioactive for the next 500 years or so."

Weed turned and walked back over to his rocking chair. He made a sniffing sound before replying. "Hmm, guess I'll hold off on that then fer a while." He slowly sat back down. "Well, Mr. President, if'n that's who ya really are. Don't take this the wrong way, but ... if'n what ya say is true, then ... we need to celebrate!"

Roger's face screwed into a frown. This wasn't the response he'd been anticipating. But he held back and said nothing. Weed raised himself back up and walked over to the left wall and opened up the cupboard. He moved things around, dug into the back and finally pulled out an old bottle. Originally there had been a paper label on the glass, but most of it was worn away. He wiped the dust off the top and then unscrewed the cap. Weed took a quick sniff and moved his nose away. "Wow! I think this baby's ready ta drink!"

He took out two clean paper cups and set them down on the counter. Then he filled them both halfway. He took one to Roger and handed it to him.

He carefully helped Roger prop himself up in bed so he could drink. The president looked down at the contents of the cup. The color seemed very strange to him.

"What is it?"

A look of pride swelled onto Weed's face. "It's Boone's Farm Wild Mountain. Vintage 1970. I been savin's this fer a long time."

Roger looked surprised. "Well, yes. I guess you have. What does it taste like?"

Weed picked up his paper cup and held it out to Roger. They clinked their waxed cardboard cups together but it made no clinking sound.

"It tastes like a mountain a grapes! An it's got lots a other natural fruit flavors too! I know cuz that's what it said on the label." He looked down at the bottle. "It's all wore off now though."

Weed raised up his cup and proposed a toast. "To the IRS. May it glow in the dark fer the next thousand years!"

Originally, Roger had no intention of drinking the contents of the cup, but when he heard the toast, a smile grew upon his face. He raised the cup slightly, and held his breath while taking a tiny sip. It burned and he almost threw up. But he forced himself to smile, all the while thinking *it tastes like unleaded gasoline ... with a fruity aftertaste.*

One of his latest election promises had been to reform and simplify the tax code. He thought to himself. *Guess I won't have to do that anymore.*

Weed quickly drained his cup. Refilled it, then guzzled it down again. "It's got a kick, don't it?"

Roger nodded. "Yes, sir. I can honestly say that I've never tasted anything quite like this before."

And then he looked around the room as if searching for something. Finally, he saw what he was looking for.

"Say, Weed. You don't by any chance have a telephone or a short wave radio do you?"

Weed smiled. "I might got one you could use."

Roger set his paper cup down on the bedside table. "So what would it take to get you to make a phone call for me?"

The old man shrugged his shoulders. "I don't know. What ya got that's worth anything?"

Roger thought for a minute. Weed still didn't understand. But he thought he knew what a man like Weed would appreciate.

"Tell you what, Weed. You make that phone call for me, and I'll have a chopper fly in a pallet of MREs, an M4 carbine with 10,000 rounds of ammo, night vision goggles, and ... " Roger hesitated and Weed leaned in closer.

"And what?"

"And I'll throw in 3 cases of wine."

Weed looked away and then turned back to his president. His face grew the biggest smile Roger had ever seen.

"Ya got yerself a deal! Let me see if the radio still works."

> *"We regard God as an airman regards his parachute; it's there for emergencies but he hopes he'll never have to use it."*
>
> – C. S. Lewis

CHAPTER 6

Mountain Home Air Force Base

"**W**HEN DID THE CALL COME in?" General Ashby barked gruffly at the lieutenant who'd reported to him. "Quick, man! I need to know."

"It was late last night sir after you'd gone to bed."

Ashby fumed his impatience. "Why wasn't I told right away?"

The young lieutenant seemed flustered and unsure about how to answer. "Well ..." He paused. "We didn't want to wake you, sir."

The Chairman of the Joint Chiefs threw the note down on his desk and jumped to his feet. "Have we confirmed the validity of this report yet?"

The young lieutenant shook his head back and forth. "No, sir."

Ashby was on his feet and moving toward the door of

his office. "So the President of the United States, who's been missing for days, calls for help, tells us he's injured, and requests a medevac, and no one tells me because I'm sleeping?" He got right up into the lieutenant's face. "Is that correct, lieutenant?" The young man stuttered, but never gave a complete answer, so General Ashby continued with his tongue lashing.

"Do you think I'm ugly, lieutenant?"

The lieutenant answered abruptly without thinking.

"No, sir, not at all."

"Then why do you think I need all this beauty sleep?"

The lieutenant suspected this was a rhetorical question and wisely remained silent.

"I want drones in the air! I want choppers combing the area! I want special ops guys all over the mountains surrounding Pigeon Creek!"

The lieutenant was in full panic mode now. He'd never met a 4-star general before, much less been dressed down by one.

"Yes, sir. I understand, sir."

And then Ashby got right up into the man's face. "I don't care what has to be done, lieutenant. I want you to find the president and bring him back to the base." He paused for effect. "I don't care how many mountains have to be moved, how may people have to die in the process. I don't care what you have to do. Somebody better squat down right now and crap me out a president!"

The lieutenant took a step back, rendered his best salute, did an about face and rushed out the door.

General Ashby turned back to his desk and smiled before walking back and reseating himself behind his cluttered desk. Normally he was a spit-and-polish kind of guy, but now, there was just too much paper on his desk, and each pile of paper represented a crisis beyond the scope and magnitude of anything known to modern man.

But still ... he smiled. They needed Roger Thornton. He was swift. He was decisive. He was a natural, born leader. And without him the country would continue to flounder. In his heart of hearts, Ashby believed that most people were sheep in need of a shepherd, and Roger Thornton was his shepherd of choice.

Pigeon Creek Diner

"I THOUGHT THAT MEETING YESTERDAY WENT PRET-ty good, Matt."

Matt was sitting across the table from Chief of Police, Luke Gibbons. His wife, Theresa, walked up to the table with a glass carafe of coffee. Matt put his hand over his mug, but Luke held his up so she could refill his cup.

"Thanks sweetie. I sure do love you."

Theresa smiled. "Well of course you do. I'm young, beautiful, and I make minimum wage plus tips." She bent down and kissed her husband atop the head. "What's not to love?"

Matt and Luke both laughed out loud. Theresa walked away, set the carafe back in the warmer and then walked over to the opposite corner of the diner where her 3-year-old daughter was playing with Samantha.

"It went well, Luke. It was a good meeting, and I think most of the people here are going to ride things out okay, but ..."

Luke picked up his mug and took a tiny sip. "But what?"

Matt shrugged. "Well, I'm a bit concerned about the food situation. We've got over 600 residents in town and not near enough food."

Luke didn't say anything at first He was pondering the point. Finally he spoke.

"Theresa put in a big order for the diner, and our family is pretty well stocked, but she's concerned that the trucks aren't running anymore."

Matt nodded. "She's right to be concerned. I doubt we'll see any more truck shipments in Pigeon Creek for a very long time." He looked out the window and shook his head back and forth. "I'm afraid that whatever food and goods Pigeon Creek has right now is all we're going to get. Because there won't be any more buying and selling in Pigeon Creek for a very long time."

Luke blew the steam from his mug and took a sip of coffee. "So, what do you think might happen when people start running out of food?"

Matt looked him in the eyes. "You're the Chief of Police. You've lived here your whole life. You know these folks better than I do." Matt looked over at Samantha playing with little Lacy. The two of them looked so happy and peaceful together that he couldn't imagine lawlessness ever coming to his little town. "Listen, Luke, I know these are mostly good people here, but ... what's going to happen when parents can't feed their kids? Are they just going to watch while their sons and daughters starve to death? Or are they going to do what has to be done to keep their kids alive?"

Luke reached up and placed his left hand under his chin. Then he stroked the day-old whiskers before answering. He'd been so busy answering calls that he hadn't been able to shave yet.

"That's a good point, and I hear what you're saying, but ... I don't know, Matt. It's just hard for me to believe that my friends and neighbors here would turn on each other."

Matt leaned back in the diner's bench seat and stretched his back. "I know. I know what you mean, but, think about it this way. Even in the best of times there are a few bad apples in Pigeon Creek and the surrounding area. What happens when the phones go out, which they will. What happens when the electricity stops flowing, when cars stop running for lack of gas? What's going to happen when the bad apples in the basket start to realize that people can't call nine-one-one. What happens when they understand that the police are no longer a restraining force."

Luke shook his head. "I'll still be here. I'll work without pay if I have to, Matt."

But Matt waved him off with his hand. "I know that, Luke, and no one's doubting your abilities or your integrity." He thought for a moment. "Remember last year when those three junkies from Boise rode through here and broke into Frank Mason's house and held him and his family hostage? That was more than you and your deputies could handle, so what'd you do? You called in the state police and the county sheriff for back-up."

Luke looked down at his coffee cup. He thought silently for several seconds. Then he looked back up again.

"Do you really think it will get that bad, Matt?"

Matt nodded without hesitation. "I know it will, Luke, and much quicker than you think." He paused. "Within a few weeks, maybe even days, people will be driving through Pigeon Creek that you've never seen before. Even as we speak the survivors of Seattle and refugees from Portland are fleeing east to get away from rampant crime and a radioactive wasteland." He met Luke's stare with one of his own. "You need a plan, Luke. And you need one fast."

Luke looked over at his daughter, then back over to Matt. "I guess you're right. It wouldn't hurt to plan for the worst."

Matt didn't want to push him too hard, too fast, but he knew in his heart what had to happen. He went lightly. He wanted this to be Luke's idea.

"So how many officers do you have right now, Luke?"

Luke pushed his mug away from him and then looked out at the passing cars on the road. The volume had increased from yesterday.

"I'm the only full-time cop, but I have three reserve officers that work part time."

Matt nodded his head "That's good. At least it's not just you."

Just then the door flew open inward and a man staggered inside. There was blood on his face and he held his left arm up against his chest.

"Luke! You in here?"

Luke jumped up, followed closely by Matt.

"What's wrong, Willard? Who did this to you?"

The old man stumbled and Luke helped him sit down at a table closest to the door. The man was breathing hard. Sam and Theresa hurried over as well.

"There's some guys down at the grocery store. They're bustin' things up and I guess I got in the way."

A look of disbelief came across Luke's face. "Why would they do that? Who are they?"

Willard spit some blood out of his mouth onto the floor. "I don't know who they are. Not from around here. They just came in and tried to buy a whole truck load of food, but Jason wouldn't sell it to them. He's limiting purchases. They got mad and just started wrecking stuff and taking what they wanted. They're down there right now loading stuff into the back of their pick-up truck."

Luke looked over at Theresa. "Honey, you take care of Willard. I gotta go down there." Then he looked over at Matt. "Can you help?"

Matt nodded. He gave Samantha a hug and quickly dashed off behind the Chief of Police.

Samantha stood dumfounded as she watched the man she loved hop into a police car and drive away with the siren blaring. Then she looked over at Theresa.

"Is it always like this in Pigeon Creek?"

WHEN THEY ARRIVED AT THE GROCERY STORE JUST A few blocks from the diner, they were met with a hail of gunfire. The bullets struck the windshield of the police SUV as well as the engine compartment. Luke jerked the wheel hard to the right and crashed into a parked car. He opened the door and jumped out onto the ground. Matt followed his lead.

"Get that body armor out of the back seat and put it on!"

Matt did as he was told while Luke popped open the back hatch. He raised a compartment door and pulled an M4 out of its foam cut-out. He slammed a 30-round magazine into the well and pulled back on the charging handle.

"Matt, the car we plowed into is giving us cover. Get back up into the front and get the shotgun."

Staying low to the ground, Matt recovered the shotgun and moved back to his friend. "What do we do, Luke?"

They could hear screaming from inside the store now as three men ran out with their arms full of groceries and began loading them into the pick-up bed. They were about 20 yards away. Just then the store manager ran after them holding a 38 revolver in his right hand. He pointed it at the men. "Put those groceries back!"

He barely got the words out of his mouth before a barrage of bullets ripped into his chest. The manager fell backwards onto the pavement and didn't get back up.

Luke found the shooter and put the red dot of his M4 onto the man's chest and squeezed off a 3-round burst. The shooter slumped down. Four other men began shooting back at the police SUV.

"Give me some cover fire, Luke!"

And then Matt ran to the front of the SUV and then sprinted out of the cover to the right of the grocery store. Luke wounded one man in the leg and he dropped his carbine. Matt was now firing from the right flank and quickly shot two more men, hitting one in the face and another in the chest. Every time he pressed the trigger, the shotgun recoil re-injured the bear attack wounds on his chest and shoulder, but he fought through the pain.

The remaining man quickly threw down his pistol and surrendered. Luke and Matt approached quickly and carefully. Only two were left alive.

"Cover me while I cuff this guy, Matt."

Matt pointed his gun at the man up near the front of the truck. He'd been shot in the leg, and his hands were lifted in surrender.

Luke then moved to the cab of the pick-up and put flex cuffs on the wounded man. Then he pushed the button on his mike and yelled into it.

"Dispatch this is Pigeon Creek. We've got shots fired and five men down. We need police back-up and emergency medical, over."

Luke finished cuffing the man and waited for a response, but none came. He tried again.

"Dispatch this is Pigeon Creek. We've got shots fired and five men down. We need police back-up and emergency medical, over."

Several residents ran out of the store now. A few of them appeared bloody and beaten. They staggered out and dropped to the sidewalk when they saw Luke.

Luke ran up to one of them and yelled in his face. "Jim, is there any more of them?"

The man shook his head. "Don't think so. Think ya got 'em all. My wife's dead. They shot her, Luke."

And then he brought his hands up to his face and cried.

Luke looked over at Matt and barked out an order. "Get over to the fire barn. There should be an EMT on duty. Get them here now!"

Just then Matt looked up and saw something floating to the ground. It was a parachute. Then he saw another and another. There were dozens of white chutes floating to the ground all around Pigeon Creek. And there were men with guns hanging beneath them.

Luke looked up and saw them too. He ran over to Matt.

"What the hell is going on?"

> *"It seems to me that trying to live without friends is like milking a bear to get cream for your morning coffee. It is a whole lot of trouble, and then not worth much after you get it."*
>
> – *Zora Neale Hurston*

CHAPTER 7

Just North of the Oregon State Line

MARVIN TUBBS LOOKED around at the arid fields surrounding him and shuddered. A few hours ago it had been in the mid-sixties, but now that the sun had almost gone down, the temperature had plummeted.

Several cars had gone by in the last hour, but no one would stop to help. Once he'd become impatient and stepped out into the middle of highway 221 to force the issue and had almost been run down. It was hard for him to judge the driver since he'd probably do the same thing in his shoes.

Alexandra opened the Land Rover door and stepped out and walked over to her husband. "You should let me try now, Marv. No one's going to stop for you. You look too intimidating."

Marvin glared at her out the corner of his eye. "I don't

know why you say that Alex. I'm a very nice guy."

Alex smiled and dropped her head down slightly, then back up again. Then she shook it back and forth. "Marvin, will you get real please? You're standing in the middle of the road holding a machine gun. No one's going to stop and help."

Marv dropped the Ruger PC-9 and let it hang on the sling around his neck. He loved the carbine, but it was way too heavy for a talkshow host.

"I told you, Alex, it's not a machine gun. It's a semi-automatic carbine."

Alex walked up and stood beside him before gently resting her head on his shoulder. "People don't know you the way I do, Marv. You should let me give it a try."

Marv shook his head emphatically. "No way, Alex. I know what type of man stops to help you. I know what men are like. If someone stops to help you then I'll just have to shoot them again."

Off in the distance, Marvin heard the sound of an approaching car. "Quick, Alex. Get over and hide behind the car. I don't want anyone to see you!"

Alex stood up straight beside him and crossed her arms over her chest in an authoritative pose. "No Marvin. Not this time. It's getting cold out here!"

The vehicle was getting closer. Marvin could see it now. It was an old pick-up truck with a bad muffler. Marvin imagined a group of redneck thugs all hell-bent on soiling the virtue of his beautiful swimsuit-model wife.

"Hurry, Alex! They're almost here! I need to flag them down."

Alex nodded as she walked back over to the Land Rover and stood behind it out of sight. The old truck came closer but didn't slow down. Its front quarter panels were rusted and just barely hanging on. The paint job was half-faded blue with some primer here and there.

Marvin tried to smile and raised a hand up in his most friendly and nonthreatening wave, but the truck didn't slow.

When the truck was about 50 yards away, Marvin watched in horror as his wife stepped out from behind the Land Rover and wave while smiling from ear to ear. The truck slowed and came to a stop right beside Alexandra. She walked up to the truck and began talking to the man inside.

Marvin braced himself for a gunfight. Then Alex yelled over to him. "C'mon, Marvin! Harold's going to help us out!" And she waved him over with both arms.

Marvin lowered his head in defeat. She was never going to let him live this down. He walked over to the truck and looked inside. The man appeared to be several hundred years old, so Marvin let the carbine drop down onto the sling. The old man smiled.

"I got a tow strap in the back, young man. Just hook it on and put the car in neutral and I'll give ya a tow."

Alex was still smiling. "Thanks so much, Harold. We really appreciate it."

Harold laughed out loud and all the wrinkles in his face seemed to tauten up and then relax again. But Marvin looked at him skeptically. "Where are you taking us?"

Alex elbowed him in the ribs. "Be quiet, Marv. Just let the man be nice to us."

The old man laughed again. "That's okay, young'n, I understand. Ya can't be too careful these days." And then he made eye contact with Marvin. His eyes were an ancient blue, and radiated warmth and kindness.

"My house is just about three miles down Sellards

Road. But you best hurry cuz Sally doesn't like it when I'm late getting home."

Marvin looked over at his wife, but she was already walking around to get in the truck with Harold. He frowned. "Okay then. I guess it's decided."

Five minutes later they were being towed down a side road. Marvin steered the Land Rover while Alex talked to Harold in the old pick-up truck. Marvin remained quietly skeptical.

Harold and Sally

"SALLY IS YOUR COW?"

Harold laughed as he sat down on the milking stool with the bucket between his old knees. He reached down slowly and grabbed onto the cow's udders before squeezing with his thumb and forefinger. White milk came out in a steady stream for as long as he pulled.

"Of course she's a cow. And she doesn't like it when I'm late for the milking cuz it's painful."

Marvin shrugged. "Yeah. I suppose. I thought Sally was your wife."

Harold paused long enough to look up at his company. "Well that's the dumbest thing I ever heard, son. Why would I marry a cow?"

Marvin started to answer but stopped himself. Instead he changed the subject.

"So how long you lived here?"

Harold went back to milking. The sound of the milk hitting the metal pail made a tinny, ringing sound until there was enough milk to cover the bottom.

"Been here my whole life, son. Born 'n raised right here in Benton County."

Marvin looked around the small wooden barn. Then he looked back down at Harold. "You mean to tell me you milk that cow every morning and every night?"

Harold nodded. "Sure do."

Marvin saw a wooden barrel over by the wall. He pointed at it. "You mind if I pull that up and sit down while you milk?"

The old man answered without stopping. "Knock yerself out, son."

Marvin got the barrel and slid it over to where he'd been standing. He sat down on it. "So what do you do with all the milk? You can't possibly drink all that by yourself."

"That's true. I give it to the family down the road. They got five kids."

Marvin nodded his understanding. "That's pretty nice of you."

"I spose." The pail was half full now and foam was rising up about an inch thick in the bucket.

"And it was pretty nice of you to stop and help us. You didn't have to. We must've had 20 cars go by us before you stopped."

Harold didn't saying anything for a few seconds. Suddenly he stopped milking. "Yer wife tells me you had to kill a man back a ways."

Marvin looked down into his lap, but didn't say anything for several seconds. Harold went back to squeezing the udders. "You don't got to talk about it if ya don't want to."

Marvin's eyes squinted. Then he looked over at the wall of the barn. The wood was bare and weathered.

"It happened kinda fast, Harold. It never happened to me before."

The milk bucket was three-quarters full now. Harold nodded as if he knew what Marvin was talking about.

"Yeah, I reckon the first one's the toughest."

Marvin sat up straight on the wooden barrel. Harold glanced over at him but didn't say anything else for several seconds. Marvin just waited.

"It's the ones from up close that get you the most." He paused from his milking as he talked. "The long-distance shots aren't so bad, especially after the first one, but ..."

He had Marvin's full attention now. "Were you in the military?"

The sound of milk streams hitting the foam started up again as Harold talked. "Army. Southeast Asia. Two tours."

Marvin stood up nervously and stretched his legs, then sat back down again. "I was over in the sand box during the Gulf War. Marines. But I doubt it was anything like Vietnam."

"Here. Take this bucket."

Marvin jumped up and grabbed the full bucket of milk from Harold. The old man stood up slowly and groaned out loud as he stretched.

"Don't be too quick to judge, Marvin. I never met a war that wasn't hell."

The two men stood side by side in the barn now. Marvin was half a head taller than Harold. The old man's frame was bent down with wear and age. The older man reached his right hand over and placed it on Marvin's shoulder.

"You understand that you'll probably have to kill again don'tcha?"

Marvin suddenly felt very tired and very old. He nodded. "I suppose I do."

Harold smiled. "Ya know that wife a yours is gonna

draw a lot of attention right?"

Marvin nodded. Harold squeezed his shoulder reassuringly. "It'll be okay though." Then he started to walk toward the barn door. "But I'd see if I could dress her down just a tad though. That woman is just too dern good looking to be traipsing around dressed to kill while all hell breaks loose."

Marvin followed him out the door. "I was thinking the same thing. But Alex seems to think her good looks are still an asset."

Harold laughed out loud. "Well, I guess time will tell. It's probably a little of both. A good woman is a sword that cuts both ways. She can save yer life or she can get ya killed."

Marvin thought about that as they walked back into the old farmhouse. Alex had dinner ready and waiting on the table. It was chicken-fried steak, peas and mashed potatoes and gravy. Marvin was quiet through most of the meal. Alex and Harold talked incessantly though. Harold seemed to have a rejuvenating effect on his wife, and for that Marv was grateful.

That night Marvin and Alexandra slept in a strange bed that was soft and comfortable. As they lay there in bed together, snuggled up warm and fairly safe, Marv couldn't help but wonder. *Are we going to get any more nights like this? Are we even going to make it back to Pigeon Creek?"* He must have been tired, because he didn't remember falling asleep ... just the sound of Alex' steady breathing and the warmth of her body wrapped up close to his own.

THE NEXT MORNING MARVIN WOKE UP FEELING REfreshed. They ate a breakfast of pancakes, sausage and eggs, and then Marvin helped Harold milk the cow. He'd never milked a cow before and it took some getting used to.

After that, Harold drove them into the nearest town to the car parts store. They didn't have the exact radiator hose he needed, so he bought three likely candidates that were a close fit. He also bought some extra belts and hoses along with a box of tools just in case something else happened. It was a small city of about 5,000 people, and Marvin was pleased to see that law and order was still operational.

When they got back to Harold's house, it took them a few hours to get the Land Rover up and running again. At 4 in the afternoon, they were ready to leave again. Harold surprised Marv when he made a request.

"Say, Marvin, you mind if I talk to yer wife alone for a few minutes?"

Marvin had grown to like the old man a lot, and he wanted to trust him, but ... it seemed like such an odd request. He glanced over at Alexandra and she smiled back at him and nodded.

"Sure. No problem." He turned toward the barn. "I'll go say my good byes to Sally and the chickens."

Once Marvin was out of hearing, Harold walked up close to Alex and put his arm around her. He wasted no time, because there was no time to waste.

"Listen, honey. I'm old enough to be your great grandfather, but I want to give you some fatherly advice if ya don't mind."

He waited and she answered right away.

"Of course, Harold. What is it?"

The old man paused, took a deep breath and then launched into his speech. He'd obviously been thinking about it for a while.

"Alex, yer a gorgeous woman and that's always been a good thing for you, but ..." He paused. "How should I say this?" He grabbed both her shoulders and lined up straight with her. Then he looked her in the eyes.

"It's not an asset anymore. It's a liability. This is the apocalypse, and men who want you will now just take you. But in order to do that, they first gotta kill Marv."

Tears welled up in her eyes, and she nodded her head. "I think I'm figuring that out."

Harold smiled sadly. "Well, you need to be careful. No more Little Miss Innocent. Ya'll can't afford it. And Marv needs you to back him up." He paused. "Do you understand what I'm tellin' you, girl?"

Alex lowered her head. "Not ... totally."

Harold got his face right in front of her own, then moved it closer to within just a few inches. "You might have to kill someone to save your husband's life."

They both heard the barn door slam shut. When Marvin walked up, Harold was holding Alexandra in a gentle embrace. The two separated. Marvin looked into her eyes and asked. "Are we good?"

She nodded and gave the old man one last hug before getting into the Land Rover. Marvin reached out to shake Harold's hand, but the old man moved in closer and gave him a hug. Marvin felt happily clumsy.

The two men stepped away.

"I gotta milk the cow now."

Harold walked into the barn without looking back. Marvin got in the car and slowly pulled out of the driveway. A few minutes later they were driving down highway 221 with the setting sun in their rear windshield.

> *"I am an Airborne trooper! I jump by parachute from any plane in flight. I volunteered to do it, knowing full well the hazards of my choice."*
>
> – *Airborne Creed*

CHAPTER 8

Pigeon Creek

"**W**HO'S IN CHARGE HERE?**"
Luke and Matt looked over at the soldier dressed in digital camo but said nothing. The man was tall and strong and seemed to hold himself at a permanent position of attention. Finally, Luke spoke as he walked toward him.

"I'm Chief of Police Luke Gibbons. This is a crime scene, and I'm trying to get medical aid and perform a criminal investigation." He paused slightly. "Who are you?"

The other man smiled. "Major Redmond Sparrow, 82nd Airborne, at your service, sir."

The major reached out to shake Luke's hand. Luke nodded and extended his hand. Matt walked up and shook the man's hand as well. There was blood soaking into Matt's shirt from his re-opened wounds.

"I thought you guys were stationed at Bragg in North Carolina."

The major frowned. "We were. But the east coast isn't very hospitable right now. Lots of radiation. We were broken up and sent to safer bases all over the country, mostly out west here. We're out of Mountain Home Air Force Base right now."

The major looked down at the dead store manager and then over at the people bleeding on the sidewalk.

"What happened here?"

Luke slung his M4 over his left shoulder before speaking. "I'm not totally sure yet, but it appears that five out-of-towners came in and tried to steal a pick-up load of groceries and killed several of my citizens in the process."

The major nodded. "Well, I'm sorry we didn't get here a few minutes sooner." He looked around at the people coming out of the grocery store.

"I can have my medics help your EMTs if you'd like. You seem a bit overwhelmed right now."

Luke forced a smile onto his face. "Thanks Major Sparrow. That would be great."

The major turned away as he barked out a few orders to a man beside him. "Lieutenant Foster, you heard the man. Make it happen!" The Lieutenant turned and strode away to carry out his orders.

The major turned back to face Matt and Luke just as the town ambulance pulled up to the scene. Two EMTs got out and started rushing around performing triage.

"Major, if you'll excuse me, I need to start my investigation. Thanks for your help." Then the Chief of Police hurried away to see who needed help. The major turned back to Matt.

"So, are you a deputy or something?"

Matt tried to smile but failed. "No, not really. I just happened to be with the Chief when people started shooting at us."

The major nodded his approval. "Well, you certainly do good work under stress." A captain came up, saluted and asked a question. The major answered crisply and the captain briskly walked away. Matt was impressed with their professionalism. He decided to try and get some information about the world outside of Pigeon Creek.

"So, what's going on outside Pigeon Creek right now, major?"

The major looked at Matt's chest and saw the bloody shirt. "That your blood?"

Matt shrugged his one, good shoulder. It hurt. "Afraid so, Major Sparrow."

"Bullet wound?"

Matt shook his head from side to side. "No. Nothing that glorious. I was attacked by a bear a few days ago, and looks like my stitches tore open."

The major smiled. "Oh, I don't know. A bear attack sounds pretty glorious to me and I'm Airborne!" He turned and started to walk away. "Follow me and I'll get someone to fix that up for you."

Matt smiled weakly. "Thanks. My name's Matt by the way." The major was already flagging down a sergeant. "Sergeant Baxter! Get me a medic over here on the double!"

The major turned back to him. "Good to meet you, Matt. You live close by?"

Matt let the butt of the shotgun drop down to rest on the ground before answering. "Yeah, just a mile up the road."

"So how long you lived here?"

Just then the medic ran over and saluted Major Sparrow. "You called for a medic, sir?"

The major nodded. "Yes." And then he pointed at Matt's bloody shirt. "Please take a look at Matt here and get him all fixed up."

The major started to walk away, but stopped and turned back to face Matt. "Please excuse me, Matt, but I have work to do." He smiled. "You folks do pretty good work around here." He glanced briefly around at the blood and carnage. "For a civilian that is." And then he walked away while the medic unbuttoned his shirt and started asking him questions about his wounds. Thirty minutes later, when the medic was done, Matt went inside the store to find Luke.

Pigeon Creek Diner

TWO HOURS LATER MATT WAS SEATED AT HIS REGU- lar table inside the diner. Samantha had been worried about him, and all the female attention was starting to grow on him.

"It's okay, Sam. I'm alright. The medics fixed me up just fine." He looked over at Theresa who was bringing him coffee. "Luke's okay, too, Theresa. He's just cleaning up the crime scene down there."

"Tell us what happened!"

Theresa poured his coffee. Matt took a big sip and burned his tongue. Theresa sat down across from him with expectant eyes. Matt launched into a detailed account of what had transpired, pausing only to answer their flurry of questions. The whole time Samantha held onto Matt's arm and leaned her head on his left shoulder. Matt didn't say so, but he liked it. He liked it a lot.

"I thought I was going to die when I heard all that shooting downtown. I was so worried about you, Matt."

Matt breathed a sigh and then slowly took a tiny sip of his coffee. He needed the jolt of caffeine right about now. He was emotionally and physically exhausted.

Just then, the door opened up and Luke walked inside followed closely by Major Sparrow. Two other soldiers walked in, one with a radio and another with his M4 hanging by its sling. Matt could see four other soldiers were posting themselves outside the door and in the parking lot. Luke looked exhausted, but the major was as fresh and strong as ever.

"Good to see you again, Matt. How's the shoulder?"

Matt smiled weakly. "Good, major. Thanks for the help."

Luke took over the introductions. "You already know Matt. This is my wife, Theresa, and Matt's fiance, Samantha."

Sam's eyebrows raised up when she heard herself being introduced as Matt's fiance, but she didn't correct Luke, and she was pleased that Matt didn't either.

Theresa stood up and offered her seat to the major, but he waved her away. "No, ma'am. Please stay seated." Do you mind if I move a table over so we have more room?"

Theresa smiled and nodded. The major looked over at his two men by the door. He didn't say anything, just gestured with his eyes at the table, and both men walked over and moved the table for the major.

When all five of them were seated, Luke was the first to speak. "Major, I want to thank you for all your help down there. I couldn't have done it without you."

The major waved him off. "It was nothing."

Theresa stood up. "Let me get you some coffee. On

the house."

The major smiled. "That would be great, Mrs. Gibbons." Then he looked back at the others. He paused as if deciding the best way to ask a question. Theresa poured him a cup of coffee and sat back down beside Luke.

"I'm on a tight schedule, and I'm already behind so I'll get right to it." He placed his right hand down on the handle of his coffee mug. "We're here on a search and rescue mission, and it's a matter of extreme national security."

Luke nodded. "Okay. I'm not sure what that means though."

Major Sparrow didn't answer right away. He just looked first at Luke and then over at Matt. Luke raised his hands up off the table and let them drop back down again.

"Listen, major, you helped us, so we'll certainly help you. What do you need?"

A broad smile spread across the military man's face. "I'm looking for a man named Joshua Gimble. Apparently he lives in a cabin somewhere near here. Can you help me find him?"

"Joshua Gimble?" Luke looked over at Matt and shrugged. "I never heard of him, and I've lived here my whole life."

The major's disappointment was obvious. "Are you sure? We got a distress call from him on the short wave and he said he was about 5 miles southeast of Pigeon Creek. I think he lives off the grid, no phone or anything. Rather a primitive mountain type guy."

Just then Matt smiled. The major looked over at him in anticipation. Matt spoke to Luke first. "I think he means Weed. You know. The old guy who lives by himself down by the Huntington Gorge."

Matt turned to the major. "He hardly ever comes into town. Doesn't even like people I think. The only reason I remember him is because he orders ammo from me, and I see his legal name on the invoice."

The major could barely contain himself. "Can you take me to him?"

Matt thought for several seconds. "I've never been there before. I just know the general area. But I could probably get you to within a half mile radius."

The major smiled. He called over to his radio operator. "Corporal Hurt. Get over here, please!" The noncom complied quickly, and soon Major Sparrow was on the radio making plans for a rescue.

Joshua Gimble

THE PRESIDENT OF THE UNITED STATES ROLLED ALL five of the dice and laughed out loud. Weed scoffed at the man's incredible luck.

"How the heck did ya do that? You got a Yahtzee in one roll!"

Roger Thornton laughed again before picking up his mug of tea. "It's because I'm the president, Weed, and the dice live to serve me."

The two men had grown to like each other over the past few days. Weed still didn't believe Roger was the president, but that didn't seem to matter a whole lot.

"Yeah. Right. I keep fergettin'. Yer the president an you kin do anything."

Roger sipped his tea. Weed picked up the dice while Roger added 50 points to his score.

"I like this tea, Weed. What kind did you say it was again?"

Weed's mumbled reply was barely audible. "Sumac tea. Made it myself."

Roger nodded his approval. "It's got a slight lemony taste to it."

Weed rolled the dice and grimaced. Roger smiled sympathetically. "Well, I guess you could go for your ones."

"I don't want no ones. I want sixes!"

Roger smiled. "Well, okay then. Roll some sixes."

Weed picked up all five dice and rolled again. He had two ones showing, but no sixes.

"I told you to go for your ones, but you wouldn't listen to me."

Weed slammed his fist down on the wood of the table. "That just ain't right! You get Yahtzee's 'n Weed gets but-kiss! That just ain't fair."

Roger smiled but refrained from laughing. He shifted his leg and propped it up higher on the pillows. The president was still in bed with his back propped up against the head board and a small sheet of thin plywood on his lap as a table. Weed rolled again but no more ones showed up. He took a measly two points for his ones.

Just then Weed lifted his head up and then glanced over at the front window by the door. "You hear that, Rog?"

Roger looked over at the window as the sound grew louder. He wanted to get up and walk over to look out but that was out of the question. Weed got up and walked over to the window. He peered out carefully. Out on the horizon, just above the trees, he saw several tiny dots get bigger and bigger. Finally, there were six dots, and they hovered in closer. The sound was thunderous now as two Apache Gunships hovered over his cabin. Of the other four Blackhawks, three stayed at 50 feet and dropped down ropes. Weed watched in awe as dozens of soldiers dropped down out of the helicopters. They hit the ground running and fanned out around his cabin with M4s raised and pointed at him. The last Blackhawk landed about 30 yards in the clearing and a single man in a black suit and tie hopped lightly out onto the ground. He started walking over to Weed's door.

Inside the cabin, Weed turned to look at Roger. He shook his head back and forth.

"I hope ta god yer the president. Cuz ifn' ya ain't then we're in a world a hurt!"

There was a knock on the door,

"Agent Delgado. United States Secret Service. Open the door and show me your hands."

Weed looked back over at Roger.

"Well I'll be buggered. Paint me orange 'n call me a punkin'!"

Roger let out a sigh of relief. "Better open it slowly, Weed. He sounds serious."

Weed walked over to the door and opened it slowly. Several dozen Airborne Rangers leveled their rifles at Weed's head. waiting for orders to shoot.

"We're looking for the President of the United States."

Weed stumbled through his next words. "Ah, okey do-key." And then he turned his head and looked back inside. "I think it's fer you, Rog."

""From the Halls of Montezuma
To the shores of Tripoli;
We fight our country's battles
On the land as on the sea;
First to fight for right and freedom
And to keep our honor clean;
We are proud to claim the title
Of United States Marine.

– Marine Corps Hymn

CHAPTER 9

Eastern Oregon

MARV AND ALEX CROSSED OVER THE state line near Umatilla just as the sun was setting. They filled up their gas tank without incident, and then got on Interstate 84 headed toward Boise. In the best of times it was an easy 8-hour drive, but these were anything but the best of times. The gunshot wound on his shoulder had scabbed over, and the only danger now was from infection. During the gas stop, Alex had cleaned and dressed the wound, liberally applying antibiotic ointment. It was sore now, but nothing Ibuprofen and a firm constitution couldn't handle.

Alex reached into the glove box and pulled out the pills sealed up in foil and plastic. She looked at them skeptically. "Why are we taking Iodine tablets again, Marv?" She frowned. "I'm not sure this is such a good idea." She glanced over at her husband. "Did you get a prescription for these?"

Marvin kept his eyes on the highway as he followed the

red tail lights of the car in front of him. "No. I got them from Matt. We need to take them to saturate our thyroid with potassium iodide so we don't soak up radioactivity."

Alex looked over at him like he was crazy. "Have you ever done this before?"

Marvin shook his head back and forth. "Nope." She said nothing in reply, just stared down at the foil packet in her hand.

Marvin kept his eyes on the road as he reached over with his right hand. "Just give me two of them. I'll go first to make sure it's safe."

Alex shook her head back and forth as she peeled off the shiny foil from the back and gave him two tablets. Without hesitation, he popped them into his mouth and washed it down with cold coffee from the truckstop back at Umatilla.

"See, dear. Nothing to worry about it."

"Hmm, I'll wait an hour just to see if you start growing a third eyeball."

Marvin laughed for the first time since crossing over into Oregon. "It's okay, honey. I know all about them and Matt's right. You should go ahead and take them so your hair doesn't fall out."

Alex jerked her head up. "My hair fall out? You've got to be kidding me!"

Marvin continued looking straight ahead. "No joke, Alex. That's what radiation poisoning does. Your hair falls out. You get nauseous. You start to vomit. Your insides turn to gelatin and then it gets really painful."

"Alright! Alright! Please stop!"

It took Alex just a few seconds to unwrap two tablets and wash them down her throat with her bottle of water.

Alex turned her head to the right and looked out the window at the darkness. She was starting to dislike the apocalypse.

Normally she enjoyed driving through the night, but not today. Usually there were just truckers on the road, hauling their freight, but not tonight. Everyone on the road right now was a refugee, fleeing Seattle or Portland or San Francisco. Everyone on the West Coast was driving as fast as they could to get as far away from the Pacific Ocean as possible. She imagined that everyone on the East Coast was doing the same thing only in the opposite direction. All of America was being compressed into the heartland, as if they were stuck between the steel inside a vice.

As they approached the city of Pendleton, the traffic slowed and suddenly became bumper to bumper. Within just a few minutes, they went from 75 miles per hour to a total standstill.

"What's going on, Marv?"

Marvin craned his neck to see up ahead. It was total darkness except for all the lights on the cars.

"I don't know, honey."

They waited for 10 minutes, then Marv opened his door and started to get out. "Stay inside honey. Let me see what I can find out."

"Be careful Marv."

He smiled. "I will. Lock the door behind me."

Marvin patted his right hand reassuringly on his Glock 19 before closing the door. Other people were also getting out of their vehicles, and he could hear doors slamming to his front and rear.

A man walked up behind Marvin and caught him by surprise. Marvin cursed himself for his lack of vigilance.

"Can you see what's going on up there?"

Marvin turned around and his right hand automatically went down to rest on the butt of his gun. The man was looking out past him and didn't seem to notice. Marvin could tell by the look on the man's face that he was no threat. He was just as confused and frustrated as everyone else.

"Can't see a thing." In the dimness, he made eye contact with the man and decided to trust him. "I'm gonna climb up on my hood. Maybe I can see more of what's going on."

The man nodded. "Sounds like a plan."

Marvin moved to the front of the Land Rover and used the brush guard to climb up onto the hood. From his new vantage point, he saw a seemingly endless line of tail lights all the way into Pendleton. The man from down below yelled up to him.

"You see any cops up there?"

Marvin climbed back down and walked over to the man who was still standing beside the Land Rover. "Nah, no cops. I haven't seen any cops in a long time. I think they all went home to take care of their own families." Then he asked the stranger a question. "Are you from around here?"

"Yeah. My exit's about a mile down. I'm less than three miles from my house." He turned his head and spit off to one side on the pavement. "Might as well be a thousand miles for all the good it does me."

The other man's hand came up to stroke his chin while he thought about what to do. "Well, guess I'll go back to my truck and think about this for a while." He turned and walked back to his truck while Marvin looked after him. There was something familiar about this man. Then he tapped his knuckles on the window. When he heard the un-locking mechanism engage, he opened it up and climbed inside.

"What's going on sweetheart?"

Marvin looked perplexed as he grabbed onto the steer-ing wheel with both hands. "No idea, honey. No strobes up there. And the backup seems to go on forever. I can't see the end to it."

He turned his head and saw the worried look in her eyes. He tried to reassure her. "It'll be okay, Alex. I'm sure it'll clear up soon." And then he turned back to the front. "We just have to wait it out for now."

Alex nodded and reached down to the storage compartment to check her phone.

"Marvin! I've got one bar!"

Marvin hurried to pick up his own cell phone as well. "I got nothing." He leaned over so he could look at her screen as she checked for messages.

"Here's something from Sam and Matt."

She leaned closer to the console so Marvin could read it along with her.

> Hope you are okay, Alex. All is well here. Your house is waiting for you. The town was attacked by vandals, but Matt and the Chief killed them. We are safe and quiet again. Please tell us where you are. Do you need us to come get you? Love you! P.S. Matt says to turn on your GPS locator so we know where you are.

Alex looked over at him. "I should text her back. Do we need them to come get us?"

Marvin thought about it for a few seconds, but then shook his head back and forth. "No. With unreliable comms, we'd never hook up. Just tell them where we are and that it's slow going. We'll be there as soon as we can." And then he added. "Better go ahead and turn on your GPS locator though. I'll do the same with my phone too."

Alex typed furiously with both thumbs before pressing the send button. "Okay, got it done."

Just then Marvin jerked his head up and looked to the

front of the column of cars. "Did you hear that, honey?"

And then the sound came again. It was like a popping noise, one after the other in a long succession. "Those are gunshots, baby."

Marvin got out of the car again to get a better look at what was going on up ahead. He heard more gunshots. They sounded like three-round bursts from an M4 carbine. He knew the sound well from his military past. And then came the endless parade of people. It was like a riot. People screamed in terror, jumped out of their cars and started running back toward the Land Rover. Marvin drew his pistol as the people kept running past him. The gunshots were getting closer now.

Marvin stared on, not knowing what to do. The same man who'd talked to him before was suddenly standing beside him again. He seemed strangely calm as he spoke. "You military?"

Marvin nodded his head. "Marine Corps."

The man smiled. "Thought so."

And then he started to back away. "Okay, devil dog. If you want to live, then follow my lead."

Just then a man limped past Marvin, trailing a steady flow of blood from his thigh onto the pavement. He took three steps past Marvin and collapsed to the road. Marvin's first instinct was to go help the man, but just then a bullet whizzed past his head and he pushed the manual over ride button to his brain. Marvin took one look back and saw the truck lights of the man behind him as he fired up his engine. The truck backed up, slamming into the car behind him and pushing it back ten feet. It then turned to the right, raced down the slight embankment, roared through a chain link fence and off into a field.

Marvin took one last look around and hopped back into

the Land Rover. He started the engine and put it in reverse.

"Marvin! What's happening?"

Just then a bullet glanced off the hood of the Land Rover. Marvin gunned the engine, throwing Alex forward into her seat.

"Buckle up, Sweetie!"

Alex screamed as they came to a stop. Marvin felt the car bump as his wheels ran over the fallen man behind him. He slammed on the brakes, and put the car in drive again just in time to see a man pointing a carbine at his windshield. Marvin didn't hesitate. He tromped his foot on the accelerator and plowed through the man who hit the brush guard and was tossed over to his right like a rag doll.

Alex screamed again and covered her face with her hands. When the Land Rover came to a stop, Marv threw it in reverse again and backed up far enough to make it through the gap in the chain link fence. He drove down the embankment, following the truck in front of him. It had a 200-yard head start on him, so he went as fast as he could without wrecking.

"It's okay, sweetie. I have a plan!"

But Alex couldn't respond to him. She was too busy bouncing around inside the cab and still screaming at the top of her lungs. After a hundred yards more, the field leveled out and Alex was able to buckle up her seat belt. Marvin slowed down. They could still hear gun fire in the distance behind them.

Marvin had caught up to the truck in front of him now, and he continued to follow at a safe distance.

"Honey, what are we doing?"

Marvin's voice remained tense. "It's okay. I know this guy. He's a local, and he knows what he's doing."

Alex started to talk again, but Marv cut her off. "Not

now, sweetie! I need to focus!"

Marvin could see streetlights up in the distance and the truck in front of him started to slow down. Marvin followed his lead. It was a blue, Ford F-250 with dual rear tires. Just short of the road, the blue truck came to a stop.

Marvin stopped as well and just let his engine idle. As he looked on, the driver's side door of the truck flew open and the man exited the vehicle. Marvin saw something large and bulky in the man's hands.

"Marvin! It's a gun!"

Marvin responded by hitting the power window button as fast as he could.

"He's going to kill us, Marvin! Do something!"

Marvin started to sing as loud as he could.

"From the halls of Montezuma. To the shores of Tripoli!"

The man with the gun stopped and listened, uncertain of himself.

"We will fight our country's battles, on the air and land and sea!"

And then the man lowered his gun and started to laugh. Alex looked over at her husband with terror and confusion in her eyes. "Marvin. How did you do that? You're not that good a singer."

Marvin put the Land Rover in park and shut off the engine. He hopped out being careful to keep his hands in clear view. But he kept singing all the while.

"First to fight for right and freedom. And to keep our honor clean."

The man stopped laughing and joined in singing with Marvin. "We are proud to claim the title, of United States Marines!"

The man took a few steps forward before stopping. He looked Marvin over and then thrust his right hand out toward Marvin.

"Sergeant Major Will Stafford retired."

Marvin thrust out his right hand as well and the two men shook hands excitedly.

"Sergeant Marvin Tubbs, Camp Pendleton from a long time ago. Pleasure to meet you, Sergeant Major!

They paused and listened to the gunfire off in the distance.

"Sounds like they're still going at it."

Marvin nodded. The man in front of him was stocky, a bit overweight with a flat top high-and-tight hair cut.

"Thanks for the extraction. I don't think I would've thought of that route."

Will Stafford looked over toward the interstate and shook his head back and forth. "What a cluster this is turning out to be."

Marvin nodded. "You got that right, Sergeant Major. It's a crap sandwich."

The other man laughed. "Yeah. A crap sandwich without the bread!"

Will glanced back at the windshield of the Land Rover. "That the missus?"

"Yeah, it's my wife, Alexandra. Thanks for helping us out."

He waved it off. "Marines gotta stick together." He pushed his AR pistol back to his right hip and let it hang from the sling.

"Listen, Marine. I think you should follow me on home. You can meet Mrs. Stafford, and we'll get you a good night's sleep, some chow and we'll help you get back on the road to your next duty station." He paused. "Sound good, Marine?"

Marvin nodded his head exuberantly. "Whatever you say, Sergeant Major!"

"We want to do a lot of stuff; we're not in great shape. We didn't get a good night's sleep. We're a little depressed. Coffee solves all these problems in one delightful little cup."

– Jerry Seinfeld

CHAPTER 10

Pigeon Creek

"**W**HAT'S GOING ON DOWN there?"

The sound of the Blackhawk helicopter was deafening, but Roger Thornton was wearing headphones so he had communication with the pilot, the medic and Agent Delgado who was seated next to him.

"That's Pigeon Creek, Mr. President. Just a tiny, little town. Nothing of significance, sir."

Roger Thornton was feeling grumpy today. His leg was throbbing. He thought hard about Agent Delgado's statement. *Nothing of significance.*

The medic had given him some medication to ease the pain in his leg and head, but he was still thinking clearly.

"Land the helicopter. I want to see for myself."

The look on Agent Delgado's face soured, and he

spoke quickly, out of fear, and not really thinking.

"We can't, sir."

Roger turned his head quickly, like a hawk that had just spotted a rabbit running on the ground as he circled above.

"Land the helicopter ... Now!"

Agent Delgado quickly back peddled. "Yes, sir. Right away, sir!"

Agent Delgado began talking into his microphone. He spoke with the Army Rangers on the ground to make sure the area was secure, then asked the pilot to land.

SAMANTHA AND THERESA WERE INSIDE THE DINER when they heard the helicopter circling overhead. Matt and Luke had been sitting at a booth eating lunch, but got up quickly and rushed out the door. Army Rangers had been all over town for the past two days as they searched for the president. Luke was grateful for all their resources and manpower. It made cleaning up the aftermath of the attack on the grocery store much easier. Just then a HumVee drove up and parked beside them. Major Sparrow hopped nimbly out of the HumVee and strutted over to Matt and Luke. Four more HumVees pulled up and several dozen Rangers piled out and fanned out in a defensive perimeter around the diner and the parking lot.

"What's going on, major?"

As he spoke, Matt pointed up at the descending helicopter. The major didn't respond. He was too busy watching his men and barking out an occasional order to his officers.

Finally, when the helicopter was touching down, he looked over at Matt and smiled. He had to yell and shield his face from the sand that was being kicked up by the blades of the aircraft.

"Fall in behind me and you'll see." They'd become fast friends with Major Sparrow over the past two days.

Matt and Luke looked at each other vacantly. They had no idea what was going on. The major started to move forward as the blades slowed and finally came to a stop. Matt and Luke strode on after the major, not wanting to miss whatever was about to happen.

When they reached the helicopter, the major stopped and stiffened to the position of attention. Matt didn't know what to do, so he copied the major as best he could. Luke just glanced around nervously.

Suddenly, the side door slid open, and a man in a suit jumped down onto the gravel of the parking lot. He looked around nervously, briefly acknowledged the major's presence, then turned back and spoke to the man waiting inside.

"All clear, Mr. President."

President Roger Thornton rose up as best he could with his splinted leg.

"Help me get him down, major."

The major cut his salute, and then stepped forward to help Agent Delgado lower the president to the ground. The president turned to Major Sparrow.

"Major, I'd like a cup of coffee, and then I'd like to talk to some civilians. Can you arrange that?"

"Absolutely, sir."

Then he turned to Matt and Luke. "Do you mind if we take the president inside the diner for some coffee?"

Luke, whose mouth was still dropped open, suddenly regained his composure.

"Ah, yeah. Sure." Then he pointed over his shoulder toward the cafe. "I'll, ... I'll go inside and make sure

Theresa is ready for what's coming."

As Luke walked away, the president turned to look at Matt. "Do I know you, son?"

Matt shook his head dumbly. "No sir, I don't think so." Then he remembered his manners and thrust his hand out. "Name's Matt Robbins. I live right here in Pigeon Creek."

The president nodded but didn't speak further to him. "Let's get inside major. I need to rest up a bit before our next leg of the journey."

A wheelchair was brought down out of the Black Hawk and soon the president was being pushed into the diner. Agent Delgado rushed ahead to clear the building before Roger went inside. A few seconds later he opened the door and signaled the all clear.

Once inside, Theresa walked up with her perpetual smile. "Well hey there, boys. Would you like some coffee?"

The president smiled immediately. He reached out his hand to her and she accepted it right away. "My name's Theresa. How do you take yer coffee, honey?"

The major wheeled Roger over to a table away from the windows. "Make it strong today, Theresa. No sugar or cream."

Theresa nodded right away and rushed off to fill the order. Matt walked over and gave Samantha a hug. Then he led her back to the president's table.

"This is Samantha from Seattle."

The president looked up and smiled. "Oh, my word. Would you look at those eyes!" Roger reached out and took Sam's hand, then leaned in to lightly kiss the top of it. "After what I've been through the past week, you are a welcome sight to behold." Then he turned to the major. "Major Sparrow, I'd like to speak with you and Matt,

Samantha, Theresa, and the good police officer over there if you don't mind."

"Sir, yes, sir."

He turned to speak with the others, but they were already moving chairs to make it happen. Just as they were all sitting down, Theresa came with the president's coffee mug. She set it down on the table in front of him along with a white napkin.

"There ya go. Mr. President."

The president smiled. "Theresa, won't you sit with us for a while and talk?"

Theresa nodded and then gave orders to Luke. "Luke, go get Lacy in the kitchen. Let her come on out here and play so we can keep an eye on her."

Luke got up and walked back to the kitchen. He returned a few seconds later with their daughter. The president's eyes lit up when he saw her.

"Mr. President, this is our daughter, Lacy. She just turned three."

The president reached his hand out to her, but the little girl shrunk back in fear. Roger laughed out loud. Then he bent down as far as he could in the wheelchair and spoke to her. "It's a pleasure to meet you Lacy." Then he looked up at the others, who were now seated all around the red Formica-topped tables that had been pushed together to make room for them all.

The president wasted no time getting to his agenda. "Tell me what's been going on around here for the past few days, please."

Matt looked over at Luke and nodded. Luke then gave the president a summary of the town, how it had been faring, the lack of supplies, as well as the shoot-out on Main Street. The president nodded his head, his face suddenly growing serious. Then he turned to Matt.

"What do you do for a living, son?"

Matt didn't quite know what to say, so he just started rambling. "Up until a week ago I hosted a podcast called *The Happy Prepper*, but ... well, I'm obviously not doing that anymore."

"The Happy Prepper?" The president's eyes sparkled. "Well now, you were a bit ahead of your time, weren't you."

Matt nodded his head before the president continued. "So tell me, Matt. Are you still happy?"

Matt glanced over at Samantha before taking her hand. "Mr. President, in the past week I've been shot at, mauled by a bear, and lost my business, but ... I have to tell you, sir, I'm the happiest man alive."

The president nodded his approval. "That's good, Matt. Really good. Our country is going to need that positive attitude of yours if we're going to make it through these tough times."

Then he looked over at Sam. His eyes softened. "Samantha. Do you know what happened to Seattle?"

Sam bowed her head for several seconds. Then she looked back up again and made eye contact with Roger. "Yes, sir, I do."

The president reached out and momentarily touched her sleeve. "I'm so sorry, Samantha. I so much wanted to prevent that, but I just couldn't do it in time."

Theresa then chimed in. "So how did you end up president? I've never seen you before."

Roger laughed out loud. "That's a fair question." And then he reached over to his right and picked the coffee cup off the table beside him but didn't yet take a drink.

"I was the Speaker of the House, the third in line of

succession when the bombs started falling." He paused long enough to sip his coffee. "President Connor was inside the White House along with most of the cabinet, and the VP had just been removed from office. So, as luck would have it, the mantle passed to me." He took another tiny sip of his coffee. "To be honest with you folks, I'm really not ready for this job. I just don't feel worthy or up to the challenge." He shrugged. "It was hard enough just being Speaker of the House."

No one spoke for several seconds, but then Matt broke the silence. "So how's my buddy, Weed doing?"

The president's face immediately began to glow at the mention of the name. "Ahhh, Weed! My good friend, Weed!" His laugh echoed around the room. "That man almost shot me out on the side of the mountain. But then he saved me and took care of me until Agent Delgado here could come get me." He lowered his head and smiled. "That man cheats at Yahtzee you know. He beat me four games in a row! I swear those dice are loaded."

And then he turned to Major Sparrow. "That reminds me. Major Sparrow. Would you be so kind as to deliver these items to my good friend, Joshua Gimble? There's no hurry, but it does need to be done."

The president took a crumpled piece of paper out of his front breast pocket and handed it to him. Major Sparrow accepted the paper, unfolded it and read it quietly to himself. Matt saw a hint of a smile spread onto the major's lips. He so much wanted to know what was on that list.

"It will be done sir. As soon as possible."

Just then Agent Delgado, who'd left the room a few minutes earlier burst in holding a sat phone in his right hand. He interrupted.

"Excuse me, Mr. President."

Roger looked up a little perturbed. "Yes, Agent Delgado?"

He handed the sat phone to President Thornton. "It's the Chairman of the Joint Chiefs, sir. It's urgent."

Roger breathed a heavy sigh and reached out with his right hand to take the phone. He paused for several seconds as if confused. Then he smiled as he remembered.

"That's right. I promoted General Ashby right before the plane crashed." He put the phone to his ear.

"General Ashby. So good to hear your voice again."

He paused. "Well, I just stopped off at the Pigeon Creek Diner to have some coffee before coming back. I've made some new friends and they are simply delightful!"

The general was speaking at length on the other end. The president's face darkened a bit. "I see." He nodded. "Oh, that is most disturbing." He took a sip of his coffee. "Well, how many warships are we talking about here?"

The president nodded. When he answered, his voice sounded relieved. "Well thank God it's only a few. I thought you were talking about an entire armada, general." He listened to the general's reply. "Well, general. As soon as they enter US territorial waters, I want you to sink them. Any means necessary." He nodded. "Thank you, General Ashby." The president laughed and then gave one final reply. "I'll be back as soon as I finish my coffee, general, and not a moment before."

He handed the phone back to Agent Delgado. He sipped his coffee again. And then he smiled. "I apologize but it seems I'm needed elsewhere." He turned to Theresa. "Ma'am, you make the most wonderful coffee and I want to thank you."

Theresa smiled and stepped up to give him a hug. Agent Delgado tried to step between them, but Roger pushed him away. "Never come between the president and a beautiful woman who can cook, Agent Delgado." The secret service man nodded and stepped back.

The president hugged Theresa and then Samantha before shaking the right hands of Matt and Luke. Then he turned to Major Sparrow. "Let's get back to work, major."

Major Sparrow wheeled the president out of the diner and everyone else followed, not wanting to miss a thing. The Blackhawk helicopter was already warming up. After the president was loaded into the chopper, he motioned for Major Sparrow to come closer. He spoke discretely into the officer's ear. The major nodded, stepped back a few paces and rendered a crisp military salute.

As the helicopter rose off the ground, Matt and Luke looked on in awe. They'd just met the president.

Major Sparrow walked over and spoke to Matt directly. "Well, Matt. You certainly made an impression."

Matt looked confused. "What do you mean?"

Major Sparrow handed him a satellite phone. Matt reached out to accept it.

"What's this for?"

"President's orders. If it rings then answer it. President Thornton wants to stay in touch with you."

Matt looked down at the phone in his hands. He didn't know what to say, so he said nothing. Sam leaned her head against his shoulder, and he put his arm around her waist as the sound of the helicopter faded into the distance.

> *"Demonstrate to the world there is No Better Friend, No Worse Enemy" than a U.S. Marine."*
>
> *— James Mattis*

CHAPTER 11

**Pendleton, Oregon**

"**T**HANKS SO MUCH FOR PUT-ting us up last night, Mrs. Stafford. We really appreciate it. And it was so nice to get a hot shower. I feel clean again for the first time in days!"

All four of them were sitting around the dining room table eating a breakfast of bacon and eggs, toast and orange juice. The two women talked back and forth, but the men just listened while they ate. Once both men were done eating, the sergeant major stood up and pushed his chair back.

"Come on, Marvin. I got something to show you downstairs."

Marvin excused himself, but the two women were talking so intently that they didn't even realize the men were leaving. Marvin smiled. His wife was a social animal by nature, and he loved that she was getting some interaction with another woman. He knew it would help her adjust to the chaos they'd been going through the past week, and help to put her in a better mood.

Marv followed Will Stafford downstairs into the basement. When they reached the bottom of the stairs, Marvin heard what sounded like voices over a radio. Then he saw the map on the wall, and realized he'd just been invited into the sergeant major's command post.

Marvin listened to the voices. They were giving updates on what was going on all across the country. Will walked right up to the map and began briefing his fellow Marine.

"We had bombs drop in Los Angeles, San Francisco and Seattle over here on the West Coast. But thanks to a big wind coming out of the southwest, most of the fallout is going up into Canada." Then he smiled. "I don't suppose the Canadians appreciate it though." And then he moved his hand over to the middle of the map. Marvin saw colored push pins in cities all across America.

Denver got hit pretty hard. Omaha too. They got a big SAC base there. Dallas down in Texas. Texas was lucky to get only one nuke. The Midwest didn't fair as well. Chicago got hit with what looks like a Russian MIRV, so that's going to be glowing in the dark for about a million years. Detroit took a small one along with Atlanta and Miami in the south. The East Coast is toast. Philadelphia. New York, DC and then West Forks."

Marvin looked up at the blue-colored pin in West Forks, Maine. "Why in god's name did they nuke a little town in Maine?"

Will shook his head back and forth helplessly. "Hell if I know, Marv. Maybe the egg got thrown off course.

Maybe somebody just screwed up. We'll probably never know, because most of the people who did this to us are now radioactive rubble."

Marvin reached up his right hand and stroked the stubble of his two-day beard. His voice took on a solemn tone as he spoke slowly to his new friend.

"So what happened to the rest of the world? Is there going to be a nuclear winter or anything like that?"

Will Stafford stepped over to a high-backed stool and sat down. He pointed to a second stool and Marvin sat down as well.

"Near as I can tell from all the chatter, we're in a world a hurt. The US mainland didn't get it so bad as the rest of the planet, and there are certainly isolated pockets that didn't get hit at all. Australia and New Zeeland got spared along with South America. The Mideast is pretty hot right now. Most of Europe is pretty much a no-man's land, including England." He reached over with his right hand and turned down the volume on the radio so they could hear each other talk. "India's fried along with Pakistan. Russia and China duked it out and pretty much destroyed each other." He looked over at Marvin. "You want some coffee, Marine?"

Marvin nodded. "Yeah, I think I could use a jolt of caffeine about now."

There was an old Mr. Coffee on a table off to the right. Will moved to it and poured them both a mug. One mug said "Death before dishonor" and the other simply "Semper Fidelis." He handed the cup to Marvin.

Marvin was the first to break the silence. "So what do you think started it all." He reached down with his right hand and grabbed onto his mug, but he didn't take a drink. He just held it, taking in the warmth, perhaps just holding on in an attempt to gird up his strength.

"Oh, hell, I don't know. There's all kinds of talk on the radio. The TVs are all down and most of the regular radio stations too. Everybody is guessing about it though." He took a small sip of his coffee. "I suppose if I had to guess, then I'd say this attack was planned, even coordinated. It just all happened too fast to be coincidental. I think North Korea, Russia and China planned this all out, then maybe Iran jumped on board so they could destroy Israel. Seems like anyone who had an old score to settle saw the opportunity and jumped on the nuclear band wagon." He put the heavy Marine Corps mug back down and it clunked on the old work bench he was using for his command post.

Marvin looked down and shook his head from side to side. "It seems so stupid. Like a waste. We had so much going for us. And now it's all gone, all pissed away and turning to ashes."

The old sergeant major smiled softly. "Yeah. I suppose that's one way to look at it, but ... I don't know. I've been expecting it for years now. That's why I set my property up the way I did. When others lose electricity, then we'll still have it. I've got good comms here, the house is heated with wood, we've been growing our own food for decades now. So, even though the world's going to hell in a handbasket around us, well ... we'll still have a fighting chance."

Marvin thought about it. He couldn't help but wonder how he and Alex were going to get to Idaho, or if it was even possible.

"I gotta ask you, Will, I know you're all set up here, but there's only the two of you. How are you and your wife going to hold out against stuff like what's going on out there right now. I mean, let's get real here. We just watched a mass shooting last night only 3 miles from here. Heck, I had to kill a man just a few days ago." He paused. "That's never happened to me before."

The sergeant major remained silent. Marvin could tell that he was making his mind up about something, that he was coming to some sort of critical decision. Finally, he stood up quickly and motioned for him to follow as he walked over to a large, steel reinforced door in the corner of the basement.

"We're not as defenseless as you might think, Marv." He punched a combination into the keypad. There was an audible click, and then he pulled the heavy door open. "Let me show you the plan."

The room was large, about 20 feet by 40 feet, and the walls were lined with shelves full of goods and supplies of every conceivable type. Marvin could tell that much of it had come courtesy of the US military.

Marvin smiled. "Let me guess. You worked as a supply sergeant for a few years."

The old man laughed. "That's true. But all of this was come by honestly. It's amazing how much good stuff the military throws away every year. All I had to do was follow protocol and fill out the proper paperwork."

Marvin took a few steps over to the nearest shelf. He saw a wooden box with big, block letters printed on the side that said "Mine, M18A1."

A smile spread across Marvin's face. He pointed to the box. "Now, Sergeant Major, I can't imagine what kind of paperwork you had to fill out to get a case of Claymore mines."

The old Marine moved the coffee mug up to take a sip before answering. "Well, let's just say that I had to get creative on that one, and the paperwork was extensive."

Marv nodded. "Yeah. I bet it was." Then he moved to another shelf and read off a big, plastic, olive drab crate. "Grenade, Fragmentation, M67." He looked around from shelf to shelf. There were boxes of body armor, pallets of MREs, night vision goggles, M16 and M4 carbines. The back corner of the room was filled with pallets of ammo in metal, olive drab containers.

Marvin finally hurst out laughing. "How the hell did you do this, Sergeant Major?"

Will didn't answer immediately. He just turned and walked back toward the door. "Let's go back and sit and talk, sergeant."

The sergeant major closed the door and re-locked it. When they were back over at the radio bench, Will spoke first. "I suppose you're wondering why I showed you all this?"

Marvin nodded. "The thought had crossed my mind."

Marvin took a drink of his lukewarm coffee and the sergeant major followed suit.

"Listen, Marv, I'll be honest with you. I'm in a bit of a tight spot here. My original plan was to have my boy and his family come live here with us, but ..." He paused a moment, lowered his head, and his next words came out choked. Marvin was surprised at the man's sudden change.

"They lived in Los Angeles, and I'm not sure they made it out in time. He's got good training, and his teenage boys are an asset as well, but truth is I'm just not sure they're still alive, much less coming here."

Marvin looked down at his coffee mug, but said nothing for several seconds. "I'm sorry, Will. I didn't know. Maybe they'll still make it here okay?"

Will nodded. "Well, that's my hope and prayer, but it's

not a sure thing." He choked back his emotions now and took on a stone-faced demeanor. "I just need a fall-back plan, and I was thinking you and Alex might be better off staying here with us." He looked down and then quickly back up again. "You'd be an asset, and it'd be helping out both of us. You're headed to Idaho, but there's no guarantee you'll make it."

Marvin looked off to the left at the bare, cement block wall beside the colored map of the United States. He didn't know what to say. He knew what Will was saying made sense. They could indeed help each other out, and he couldn't imagine that Matt was any better prepared in Idaho than Will was here. A big part of him wanted to say yes. He'd be here with a solid, experienced, battle-hardened Marine. And the Marine Corps bond meant a lot to him. They were bloodbrothers in that regard.

He looked down at his half-full coffee cup. But ... and then he thought of Alex. Her parents were probably dead, and her only living relative was waiting for her in Idaho with Matt. He hesitated. Then he looked over to Will and made direct eye contact.

"I can't, Will. But I thank you."

The older Marine was visibly disappointed. But he was still a Marine, so he took a sip of his coffee and stood up abruptly. He seemed to shake off the bad news with ease and then took out a pad of paper and began to write.

"Well, okay then. That settles it. You understand I had to try."

Marv nodded his head, "Yes, and I'm honored. I wish I could stay."

Will began to write on the yellow legal pad. "Here is the best route for you to take into Idaho. Stay away from Boise. Lots of beaucoup bad guys there. It's bedlam and no police are functioning. Take the back roads."

He finished writing, ripped off the paper and handed it to Marvin. Marv took it, looked down at it, then folded it up and placed it in his front, breast pocket. When he looked back up, there were tears forming in his eyes, but he pushed them back and cleared his throat before speaking.

"I ... uh ... Sergeant Major, I, just don't know what to say."

Will stood up and pushed his coffee mug away. "Talk is cheap, Marine and daylight's burnin.' We need to get you on the road. Your best chance of getting to Idaho is to head out now." And then he wrote on the legal pad again. "Here's my call sign and frequencies. You don't hesitate to call if you need me. If I can help I will." He handed the paper to Marvin and he slowly accepted it.

"You know I can never repay you for your kindness."

The sergeant major laughed smugly. "Forget it. We're both Marines and we don't keep a balance sheet. Nothing owed."

He pointed toward the stairs. "Listen, head on upstairs cuz I got a few things to do down here before I see you off. Tell my wife you're leaving ASAP and she'll fix you some food to take. I'll be up in 15 minutes."

Will turned around and Marvin slowly made his way back upstairs.

An hour later, they were standing beside the Land Rover, getting ready to head out. Will had topped off their fuel tank and strapped two Jerry cans of gas on the back bumper. His wife was standing beside Alex and the two women were crying. They'd become fast friends, but the reality was, they'd probably never see each other again.

Just then Will walked out the front door carrying a

large, olive drab plastic footlocker. Marvin could tell it was heavy, so he rushed over to help him. Will shooed him away. "Get back, Marine. I might be old, but I'm not helpless." Marvin smiled as Will put the footlocker in the back seat of the Land Rover.

He looked over at Marvin and smiled. "Just a few trinkets, courtesy of the United States Marine Corps. I hope you never need them though."

Marvin stepped forward and thrust out his right hand. The two men shook and then Marvin opened the front, passenger-side door. Alex hugged her new friend one, last time, then got inside the car. Marvin slammed the door and then got in as well.

As Sergeant Major Stafford watched on with his arm around his wife, Marvin started the Land Rover and backed out of the driveway.

He tried not to look in the rear-view mirror, but he did so anyways. Will and his wife were still standing there, staring after them. Marvin looked over at Alexandra. "Are we doing the right thing, honey?"

Alex sniffed and then wiped her nose with a wet wipe from her purse. She nodded her head.

"Sam is waiting for me. She needs me to be with her."

Marvin nodded. "Of course. You're right. Family is more important than ever right now."

They reached the main road and turned right, wondering ... what is going to happen to us now?

18 The Lord God said, "It is not good for the man to be alone. I will make a helper suitable for him."

Genesis 2:18 (NIV)

CHAPTER 12

Pigeon Creek, Idaho

THE VERY NEXT DAY, MATT SAT IN church beside Samantha, listening to the eulogy for those killed in the grocery store robbery. He had his arm around Sam as he listened. There were about 50 people in the auditorium. Some were crying, but most had been shocked and stunned into a dry-eyed stupor. So much had happened in so short a time, life had changed so much that no one really knew how to handle it, how to process it, how to make sense of all the things going on in Pigeon Creek and across the planet.

After the funeral service, everyone walked out to the back side of the church property for the burial. Three townspeople had died that day, and all were interred via the same service for efficiency. That never would have happened during normal times.

The weather was nice for late October with the sun

shining and mild temperatures. Snow hadn't yet fallen, and probably wouldn't for a while. Matt was glad of that. They hadn't heard from Alex and Marvin since yesterday, and he was more concerned than ever. If they were to have an early snowstorm here in the mountains, with no snow plows to clear the roads, then Alex and Marvin would be trapped where ever they were until spring.

The burial was quick and solemn. As Matt and Samantha were walking away, Pastor Goodard approached them from the side.

"Hey Matt. Can I speak to you for just a minute?" Matt stopped and so did Samantha. "Hi Samantha. Good to see you again." Then he paused a moment. "I heard that your sister and brother-in-law are on their way here."

Samantha nodded. "Yes, they are. But we haven't heard from them today. We're pretty concerned about it."

The pastor nodded his head and he looked concerned as well. "Yes, that makes sense. Things are pretty crazy out there right now. I hope they make it here soon." And then he turned his head away as if thinking. "Perhaps ... perhaps we should pray for their safety right now?"

A light smile moved over Sam's face and then she nodded her head. She looked over at Matt to get his thoughts, but he said nothing. She turned back to Pastor Goodard with a full smile on her face. "I think I'd like that, pastor."

Pastor Goodard moved a step closer, placing his right hand on Matt's shoulder, and his left hand on Samantha's before beginning to pray out loud.

"Dear, Lord God, Almighty, Creator of the universe. Please protect and guide Marvin and Alexandra as they journey here to Pigeon Creek. Give them wisdom and courage as they travel. Lay out a clear path for them, and bring them safely home to us."

Sam looked up, but Matt and the preacher were still bowing their heads with eyes closed. She quickly closed her eyes and bowed her head. She mulled his words over in her mind. *Safely home to us.* And then it hit her. Seattle was no longer her home. Seattle was a wasteland of radioactive rubble and dust. Pigeon Creek was her home now. And then she smiled. Matthew Robbins was her home. Where ever he was, that was where she wanted to be, now and forever, and unto ages of ages.

"In the name of the Father, the Son and the Holy Spirit ... Amen."

Matt said amen so Samantha copied him. She was still new to all this religious protocol. The pastor looked up and met Matt's gaze.

"So, what's up, Pastor?"

The pastor squirmed nervously and Matt narrowed his eyes just a bit. It wasn't like him to be nervous around him. He waited for him to speak.

"Well, I'm not sure about how to go about this, so I'll just launch into it." And then he let out a deep breath. "The thing is ..." And now Matt was getting nervous. "Well, the thing is ... you and Sam aren't married and you're living together."

Matt turned his head to the side, like a rooster eyeing a potential threat. "Excuse me?"

The pastor looked down and then back up again. "Well, Matt, Sam's been here for several days and we don't have a motel, so I know she's been staying with you. Your relationship isn't platonic as I can see, so ..." He threw both his hands up at his sides. "People are talking behind your back, Matt."

At first Matt was angry, but the more he thought about it, the more he saw the point. He looked over at Samantha, but she was frowning. She spoke her mind.

"So why is that any of your business, pastor?"

Pastor Goodard looked over at the men burying the open graves and sighed in resignation. Finally, he answered her.

"Well, that's a good question, Samantha. And here's my answer."

Matt reached over to put his arm around Sam, but she stepped away from him. "Well, I can't imagine how you might answer that question, pastor, without first an apology for prying that is."

The pastor looked at Matt, then back at Sam. No one was smiling now. In the distance, they heard a truck start up and then slowly drive away.

"Okay, well... here it is. Sam, things in Pigeon Creek are different than in Seattle. God tells us in the Bible that as Christians, we should not involve ourselves with sexual immorality. We believe the Bible to be the direct Word of God, so, when The Bible tells us to do something, then we do it."

Matt's face turned beet red, and he felt the heat rise up into his cheeks. He was angry, but he also was embarrassed. "Pastor, you need to understand something. Sam and I are sleeping in separate beds, and we've done nothing together physically that we wouldn't do in front of you and the church."

The pastor put his hands deep down into his pockets and squished his fingers together over and over again.

"Well, that's good to know, Matt, and I believe you. But here's the thing. The Bible also tells us to abstain from all appearance of evil, and when the two of you live in the same house unsupervised ... well ... what does it look like?"

Samantha's anger burned out of control now. "I'll tell you what it looks like! It looks like we love each other! And isn't that what the church is all about? Love? Why shouldn't we live with each other? I love him and he loves me? And it's none of your business anyways!"

She turned and marched away in a fit of anger. Matt stood there, looking first at the pastor and then at Sam as she walked away. Finally, he threw up his hands in exasperation and yelled at him.

"You couldn't have found a better way to do this, pastor?" He stepped closer to him and the pastor backed away. "I love that woman, and I want to marry her. I can't imagine living without her. To be quite honest with you, I just haven't been thinking about the finer protocols of appearance and morality these days. I just got in a shoot-out with two men and killed them both." Then he got right into the pastor's face. "Millions, maybe billions of people are dying all across the globe and this is what's bothering you the most? You've got to be kidding me!"

The pastor didn't say anything. He just stood there with head lowered. The sound of a shovel hitting a rock clinked off in the distance in the cemetery. The pastor bowed his head. "Matt, hey, you know I love you. And please forgive me if I didn't do this in the best way. It's just ... well, it's just that I've never had to have this talk with anyone before. I know you're a good man, and that you want to please God, but ..."

Just then Matt felt Samantha's hand touch his arm. Matt was startled and jerked his head around. He saw the serious look on her face and met her gaze. Her silver-blue eyes were sparkling, no longer angry, but full of love and compassion.

"Matt, did you just say that you love me? That you

want to marry me?"

Matt looked around to see if a crowd was forming, but the three of them were all alone in the graveyard now. He nodded. "Yes, Sam. I love you and I want to marry you. I love you and I can't imagine living another day without you by my side."

The pastor cocked his head to the left. He looked first at Matt, then at Sam. Then a wind gusted and blew some leaves up and swirled them around.

Samantha smiled and leaned her head onto Matt's chest. "Then ask me to marry you."

Matt's anger faded, then he placed both his hands on her shoulders and moved her back just a tad so he could look her full in the face. Then he surprised everyone, even himself, by getting down on one knee and holding lightly onto her hands. When he spoke, it was softly and tenderly.

"Samantha Vanderveen. I love you. Will you please marry me?"

Samantha started to cry and fell down onto her knees beside Matt. They embraced and cried in each other's arms. The pastor stood there clumsily, feeling out of place, like he was interrupting an intimate moment that should be left private. Sam spoke through choked tears.

"Yes, Matt. I will marry you."

For almost a minute, Matt and Sam held each other and cried. Then, without another word, they got up and walked out of the cemetery, arm in arm, up the hill and back towards Matt's cabin.

Pastor Goodard stood alone now, in the graveyard, not knowing what to think. And then he asked himself.

"What just happened? Did I do a good thing ... or a bad thing?"

He shook his head from side to side. "Lord have mercy!" And then he walked the 100 yards to the parsonage, so he could talk to his wife about it as romance had never been his forte.

The Chinese Incursion

MAJOR CHAO LAN WAS A GOOD COMMUNIST, DEDI-cated to the party and to his country. He would rather die a painful death than fail in his mission or bring disgrace upon the People's Republic of China. Chao had been born into a good family by Chinese standards. He was intelligent, hard-working and resourceful in all he set out to do. But perhaps the trait that best equipped him for his present task was his indomitable zeal to succeed. Chao was like a giant pitbull, and once given a mission, he never stopped until it was completed.

Chao commanded an elite Special Operations unit which had been tasked with delivering the final judgement on America. Their ship had left port just as the missiles had begun to fly and the bombs had begun to fall. Their orders were to proceed to the American West Coast and carry out the attack. They were approaching the Oregon coast now, but he'd lost contact with his superiors in Beijing.

Chao looked over the railing of the fishing trawler and into the Pacific Ocean. He'd been throwing up for days, but was just now getting used to the rocking of the ship as it rose up the swell and then plunged back down into the trough. He'd always hated the ocean. The trawler wasn't real big, just big enough to be seaworthy and make the trip from China to America, but small enough to go un-recognized by the United States Navy. There were only 12 people on board. The Captain and his crew of three others, two nuclear engineers, and the major and his five soldiers. The major's sole purpose was to ensure they carried out their mission, no matter what else may occur. The sun was just coming up on the horizon now, and even a landlubber like Major Chao had to confess to its beauty. He'd been listening to the radio ever since their departure, so he knew all about the bombings across the planet. And he began to wonder if he should go through with his assignment. What was the point?

Chao thought about his wife and child still in China. His little boy would be three years old today. But was he even still alive? What about his wife? Chao had spent time in America, and he knew in his heart that not all Americans were slothful, lazy and immoral, even though the party routinely and vigorously disseminated that belief. To be sure, America had gone downhill as a culture in the past 50 years but that was to his advantage.

And he wondered about his superiors. *Are they even still alive? And, if they're not, then why should I carry out their orders?*

And then his thoughts went back to China, to his wife and child, to his mother and father. He wanted to believe that they were still alive, but ... he couldn't bring himself to think on that irrational a scale. Chances are ... they were all dead.

And that thought, suddenly gave him a clarity of mind that no other thought could achieve. His entire family, everyone he loved, was now dead. The People's Liberation Army wasn't communicating with him. He no longer had any tangible connection to his roots. And again he had to ask himself, *Why am I still fighting?*

But then he pushed the idea back down into the bowels of his soul, and promised never to entertain the thought again. It was treasonous to do so.

While the rest of his men began to wake up and begin their morning routine, Major Chao went to the wheelhouse to listen to the radio some more. He put on the headphones, and scanned the normal frequencies, but most of them were silent. Then he tried again to contact Beijing, but it was still silent. Nothing but static.

After 15 minutes, he checked in with the Captain of the trawler and then went to eat breakfast with his men. But despite his earlier promise not to question his orders, he still couldn't get the nagging question out of his mind. Why am I here? Where is my family? How will I get back home? Do I still have a home?

He ate his meal in silence, knowing all the while, that his men must be harboring the same misgivings.

39 He got up, rebuked the wind and said to the waves, "Quiet! Be still!" Then the wind died down and it was completely calm.

Mark 4:39 (NIV)

CHAPTER 13

Near the Oregon-Idaho Border

"**M**ARVIN, STOP AT THE NEXT gas station, I have to go to the bathroom."

Marvin let out an exasperated sigh. "Can't you hold it, Alex? We haven't been on the road that long. Can you at least wait until we need to fill up with gas?"

Alexandra turned toward him and gave her husband a look that would've destroyed the death star with one, cataclysmic explosion. "No, I can't hold it, Marvin! Now, please, just stop at a gas station, so I can get this done!"

Marv knew it was neither a plea nor a request. It was an order. "I'll look for a safe spot at the next town. I just don't like making unnecessary stops. I don't think we're going to be safe until we make it to Pigeon Creek."

She snapped back at him. "Well, I assure you, Marvin, that this stop is necessary unless you want a terrible mess on the front seat here."

Marvin thought about it before answering. There was so much running through his mind right now, and he was having trouble sorting it all out. He'd tried discussing it with Alex, but ... he didn't know ... she just didn't seem sympathetic to his plight. She had no idea what is was like to take a human life, and it was like she wanted to deny everything that was going on around them.

He still couldn't get the image out of his head of the man he'd shot on the roadside near Yakima. He hadn't seen a dead body since his deployment to Iraq, and, even then, he'd been spared most of the emotional trauma that other combat vets had gone through. He could still see the man's dead eyes staring up at him, like they were accusing him of the world's most unpardonable sin. And then Alex had reinforced that notion when she'd yelled at him after he'd dragged the body into the ditch. He thought to himself, *what else was I supposed to do with it? Leave it in the road for someone to run over?*

The brief talk he'd had with Harold in the barn while milking Sally had been helpful, and Marvin just wished he could talk more with someone who'd understand. He shrugged it off. For now, he'd just have to suck it up and stuff the feelings down inside him, at least until they reached Pigeon Creek.

For the most part, he didn't care how often they stopped to use the bathroom, but, deep down inside, Marvin knew that every stop they made was an opportunity for someone to hurt them, and he just didn't want to have to deal with it anymore. He didn't want to die, and he didn't want his wife to die. But he also didn't want to have to shoot someone else. And the best way to accomplish that was to avoid all people.

"There's a town coming up, Marvin!"

Marvin nodded. "I see it, honey."

It was a small town, population 983 according to the village limit sign. That made Marvin feel better as the smaller towns seemed to have more friendliness and civility left inside them.

"There's a Shell station, Marv! On the left!"

Marvin slowed and then scanned the pumps for trouble. Then he looked through the big, glass windows and saw a man standing behind the counter inside. Marvin pulled up to the pump and coasted to a stop.

Before he could stop her, Alex opened the door and jumped out and ran toward the station.

"Alex, wait!" But she kept running and soon disappeared inside the door. Marvin jumped out quickly and followed her inside just to make sure she was safe. As soon as he walked through the door, he looked to the back corner of the small station and saw the door to the bathroom closing slowly. He sighed in relief.

He looked around him cautiously. It was an old building, very small, and smelled musty and damp with other odors mixed in that he didn't recognize.

"What can I do for ya, mister?"

Marvin turned to the cashier and nodded. He was an older man, and there was a 44 magnum revolver strapped to his right side. Marvin glanced down at it, then back up again. Marvin's Glock 19 was concealed by his sweat shirt. He nodded back to the man.

"My wife just had to use the bathroom, but I might as well top off my tank while I'm waiting."

The old man smiled. "Not a problem. The tanks are turned off right now, but I can turn them on after you've paid me."

Marvin glanced out toward the pumps. Another car had just pulled in. He eyed it suspiciously and so did the clerk.

"That's okay. I can just pay at the pump."

The old man shook his head. "Sorry, man. The computers are down. Gotta be cash or nothin'."

Marvin breathed in a heavy sigh and reached back to get his wallet. He pulled out a 100-dollar bill and extended it out to the man. "I'll just come back in and get the change after I've filled up. I just need about 5 gallons."

The old man shook his head again. "Not today. It'll be one hundred for the fill up."

Marvin's anger flared up immediately. This man was taking advantage of the chaos by jacking up his prices.

"The sign out front says it's a lot less than that."

The man smiled. "Don't matter what the sign says. Matter's what I say. And I say a hundred bucks to fill that Land Rover. You look like you could afford it."

Marvin let his anger subside. They probably had enough gas to make it to their destination, but ... what if they got lost or had to detour? And then he reasoned to himself *Can I really have too much gas right now?* He finally nodded his head to the clerk. If what Matt had told them was all true, then money would be worthless in just a matter of days anyways.

"That's fine. Keep the change."

Just then a man yelled from the parking lot. It was loud and forceful. "Hey old man! Turn on the pumps!"

They both looked out and saw a very large man holding the gas nozzle in his right hand. He was gesturing toward them with his other hand by pointing down to it.

"Turn it on, Geezer!"

The old man reached back and pushed a lever. Then he

124

turned back to Marvin. "Yours is on. His ain't. Tell him to come inside and pay first if he wants gas."

Marvin didn't want to argue, so he just nodded his head and walked out, wishing all the while that his wife would hurry up in the bathroom.

When he reached the pump, he opened his gas cap, picked up the nozzle and listened to it thrum to life. He started pumping, while the other man replaced his nozzle to the pump and walked over closer to Marvin. Marvin saw two other men inside the car. They were both looking over at him.

"How come your pump works and mine don't?"

Marvin kept pumping his gas as he answered, all the while keeping the man in his peripheral vision.

"Oh, not a big deal. The guy just made me prepay. Go on inside and he'll take care of you."

The man's frown got bigger. He focused his gaze on the clerk inside, then he looked back to his car and nodded his head to the two men inside. Marvin watched it all with growing apprehension. The two men got out of the car and waited while the first man walked inside the gas station.

Just then the nozzle clicked, signifying that the Land Rover was full. Marvin replaced the cap and put the nozzle back into the pump. As he turned back toward the gas station, he heard yelling.

"I don't got no cash!"

There was a muffled reply that he couldn't make out, but he assumed it was the old man holding firm as he'd done with Marvin.

"Just run my card old man before I gotta hurt ya!"

Marvin hesitated. He wanted to go in and get his wife, but he didn't want to leave the Land Rover unguarded and he didn't feel too keen on inserting himself into the argument either. He decided to let it play out.

While he looked on, one of the men outside reached in through their open window of the back seat and pulled something out. It was a very large metal ball bat. Marvin backed up instinctively. Once he regained his composure, he moved to the other side of his Land Rover, putting it between himself and the ball bat.

The man with the bat spoke directly to Marvin now. "Just stay where ya are, buddy and mind your own business so's ya don't get hurt."

Marvin nodded his head in compliance, but kept his hands down near his waist. All of a sudden, he no longer wanted Alex to come outside. He prayed under his breath, *Stay in the bathroom, honey. Stay inside, please.*

Just then a gunshot rang out, followed quickly by a very large BOOM. Marvin's gaze jumped over to the gas station door. The door opened quickly and the large man ran out, holding his side as it trailed blood onto the cement.

"Jerry! I been shot! Help me, man!"

Jerry dropped the ball bat and ran over to help his friend. The other man drew a pistol and pointed it at Marvin. "Don't move, buddy or ya die!" Marvin didn't move.

The man named Jerry kneeled down beside his fallen partner in crime and examined his wound. It was a 44 magnum round to the stomach with a huge exit hole. Part of his intestines were hanging out onto the cement. Jerry tried to stand up, but his friend wouldn't let go of his arm. "Don't leave me here, guys! I need a hospital! Help me!"

Jerry shook his head back and forth as he yelled to his buddy. "He's a dead man, Phil. We gotta get outta here!"

Jerry tried to get up again, but the injured man still wouldn't let go of him. "Let go a me, man!"

And then he pulled out a 38 special revolver, placed it against his friend's head and pressed the trigger. The man's head jerked back and smacked hard against the cement driveway.

Jerry jumped up and ran over to his car. "Come on Phil! We gotta go!"

But Phil kept his pistol aimed at Marvin as he replied. "Our tank's empty, man! We won't get far." And then Jerry looked over at the Land Rover. "This one's full. We'll take this one."

Both men smiled like wolves that had just brought down a young deer. They pointed their guns at Marvin who had no choice but to raise up his hands in surrender.

Out of the corner of his eye, Marvin saw the gas station door open up slowly. He glanced over and saw his wife holding the store clerk's revolver up in a two-handed grip, using the door frame for cover. It was so heavy, that she had to rest it up against the door frame.

"Let my husband go!"

Jerry and Phil looked over in disbelief at Alex and the 44 magnum revolver. Their initial fear was soon replaced with a look of entertainment when they saw it was just a woman. Jerry laughed as he aimed his gun over at Alex.

"It's just a girl, Phil." And then he took a step toward her with his pistol raised up. "She can barely hold the damn thing up! She won't hit anything."

Phil still had his pistol pointed at Marvin. "Just shoot her and let's get outta here, man!"

But Jerry had other ideas. He shook his head from side to side. "No way, man. This wench is gonna be my new, best friend." He glanced over at Phil. "Just shoot her old man and we'll take the woman with us!"

Alexandra's hands were shaking hard, but when she heard those words, she tried harder to focus. And then she heard a voice in her head. It was Harold, the old man from the farm. She heard his voice as clearly as if he was there, standing beside her.

"Alex, yer a gorgeous woman and that's always been a good thing for you, but it's not an asset anymore. It's a liability. This is the apocalypse, and men who want you will now just take you. But in order to do that, they first gotta kill Marv."

Alex nodded her head, and then everything inside her became calm. It was as if the wind had been raging with thunder and lightning all around, and then ... everything suddenly became still. The world slowed and her hands stopped shaking. She took aim, and Alex pressed the trigger.

The gun jumped in her hand and flew back, hitting her in the face before dropping to the floor. A split second after she fired, Marvin moved to one side as he drew and fired 5 rounds into the man called Phil. He stood for a few seconds, then his gun hand wavered, before his grip weakened. The gun fell to the cement, followed quickly by Phil himself.

Marvin pivoted to his right, pointing his Glock at Jerry, but he was gone now. He searched quickly for Alex, and saw her crumpled onto the cement with blood flowing down the front of her face. He rushed over toward her. That's when he saw Jerry's body on the drive with half his face gone.

He ran up to Alex and kneeled down beside her. "Honey, are you okay?"

Alex looked up, and Marvin could see the laceration

where the gun's hammer had hit her in the forehead. He reached over to hold her with his left arm. He holstered his pistol and then laid her down on the floor of the gas station. Marvin pulled off his sweat shirt and pushed the cloth hard against the cut. She struggled against him.

"No, Alex. Calm down. Just relax. It's all over." Marvin laid her head on his knees as he held her in his arms. "It's okay, baby. Just relax. It's not too bad. It's gonna be okay."

Alex stopped struggling and just cried on his knees. Marvin looked over at the house across the road and saw a man step out onto his front porch. He was holding a shotgun in his right hand, but it remained pointing down. He seemed content to watch from a distance. Marvin didn't know what else to do, so he just waved in as friendly a manner as the situation allowed.

"Honey. We gotta go."

Alex tried to stop crying. "They killed the old man."

"I know sweetheart."

"They were gonna kill you too, Marv!"

He made a shushing sound with his mouth. "I know baby. But they're gone now." He moved the sweatshirt off her face and the bleeding had lessened considerably. It was a shallow wound.

"Let's go, Alex." He lifted her up onto her feet, and then helped her over to the Land Rover. Once she was inside, Marvin ran around to his own door. Before getting inside he yelled over to the man across the street. "They shot the clerk. We gotta go!"

The man nodded his understanding and watched from his porch as the Land Rover fired up and raced away. He looked over at the dead bodies before walking back inside, and locking the door behind him.

16 But Ruth replied, "Don't urge me to leave you or to turn back from you. Where you go I will go, and where you stay I will stay. Your people will be my people and your God my God. 17 Where you die I will die, and there I will be buried. May the Lord deal with me, be it ever so severely, if even death separates you and me."

Ruth 1:16-17 (NIV)

CHAPTER 14

Pigeon Creek

DEACONESS **M**ILDRED CAME TO live with Matt and Samantha, at least temporarily until they were married. She was the church-designated chaperone so to speak, and Samantha just didn't know what to think about that. She'd never heard of anything like this before, and her friends in Seattle would have laughed at her present life ... but ... she thought about it for a second ... her friends were all dead. They'd stayed in Seattle, and the once-proud and beautiful city was now a radioactive and barren wasteland.

If she didn't love Matt, she'd never agree to live this way, with a chaperone. And she thought about it now, as she stood beneath the pine tree in his front yard. The way she was living right now was antithetical to anything she'd ever known or believed in. She'd become a Christian so she could live happily ever after with Matt, and she couldn't help but wonder if she might be cheating, that she wasn't doing the whole Christian thing correctly.

She bowed her head now and prayed, something she never would have done in Seattle.

"Okay, God, if you're really there, and if you can hear me, please grant my wish. I just want to be happy with Matt. I want a family. I want him to hold me and love me and take care of me." And then she paused. "Am I Being too selfish?" And then it occurred to her that a month ago she never would have even asked that question, because for the whole of her life she'd been a selfish being, that she'd always thought of her own happiness before anyone else's, and that if a person or a place or a thing didn't add to her own happiness, then she'd always been quick to purge it from her life. And then she found herself thinking the oddest thing. *It's true. I am a selfish person.* So she looked up at the blue sky, with scattered white clouds up high, and then up into the green pine boughs.

"Jesus ... I'd like you to make me more like Matt. He loves people. He cares about everyone, and I want to be like that too."

And that was the end of her prayer. At the time she didn't realize the chain of events that it might catalyze, or else she may have been more hesitant to call upon the Lord, but ... she just flat out didn't know any better. The Creator of the universe was new to her. She was simple in the ways of all things God, so her prayers were simple as well.

Just then the door of the cabin opened up and Mildred walked over to the tree and stood beside her.

"Good morning, child. How are you today?"

Sam didn't really like the way Mildred talked. It seemed so formal and alien to her, like something out of the nineteenth century.

"Oh, Hi Mildred. How are you?"

The older woman smiled. "I'm doing well, but you didn't answer my question. How is beautiful, young Samantha today?"

Sam had just met this woman yesterday, and she still didn't know how she felt about her. She thought about the woman's question and the way she said it. She still wasn't used to people actually caring about how she felt. She sighed and looked back up at the mountainside. It was the prettiest green.

"I brought you something warm, young lady." Mildred lifted the red, flannel, long-sleeved shirt to her shoulders and Sam accepted it willingly. She felt the soft cotton and smiled.

"This is Matt's shirt."

Mildred smiled softly. "Yes, I thought you might like wearing something that he wears, since you love him so much." And then there was an awkward silence as Sam buttoned the shirt in front of her. Finally, she spoke her mind.

"This is a very strange town, Mildred."

The old woman took a step closer. "Please call me Millie. All my friends do."

Sam nodded. "Okay, I guess I can do that."

Millie folded her arms across her chest. She was shorter and rounder than Samantha. "Yes, I suppose it is strange, especially when you compare it to Seattle." She paused a moment. "I used to live in Seattle, you know."

Sam looked over at her, surprised at her statement and amazed that the old woman had ever lived anywhere except Pigeon Creek.

"Oh really? What part?"

The woman looked up at a passing cloud and watched it drift by as she spoke to her.

"North Queen Anne, if you know where that is."

Sam turned to her and smiled. "Yes, of course. I lived not too far from there. I used to pass through Seattle Pacific University all the time. They had the nicest little coffee shop there. Is that where you mean?"

The old woman looked over at her. "Yes, exactly. That's where I went to college."

Sam's brow furled down as it tightened. "You went to college?"

Millie laughed out loud. "Well, of course, dear. I was in the electrical engineering program there. After graduation, I worked in Seattle for five years before I met my husband, Ray."

Sam was astounded by this new information. "Oh, I just thought ..." But she didn't finish her sentence. Millie finished it for her.

"You just thought that everyone who lived up here in the mountains was a hick and didn't know anything about anything important?"

Sam wisely kept her mouth shut.

"Oh, it's okay, Sam. I felt the same way when I moved here to Pigeon Creek. It's natural to feel that way. People from the city think country folks are uneducated and backwards, and people from the country think city slickers are decadent and snooty."

Sam thought about that for a while before saying anything for fear of offending her new friend. And then she nodded her head up and down slowly.

"Okay, yeah. I guess you got me on that one." She looked up again at the cloud. It was almost over the mountain peak now. "So why did you give up your engineering career and move to Pigeon Creek?"

Millie smiled and put her arm around the young woman. "For the same reason you did. Sam."

Samantha looked a bit confused. "I moved here because Seattle was destroyed by a nuclear bomb."

Millie squeezed her shoulder gently. "Sure ya did, sweetheart. Sure ya did."

Samantha frowned and tried to pull herself away. "I didn't move here to be with Matt!"

"Of course you didn't. But I never said you did. That would be a sign of weakness."

Sam scoffed at her. "That's right! I don't need a man to make me happy. I'm an independent woman! I'm strong!"

Millie suddenly dropped her left arm from around Sam's shoulder and turned to face her. She looked her full in the eyes.

"Listen, sweetie. Needing a companion in life doesn't make you weak. Denying what you need is what makes you weak." And then she turned back to the right, toward the driveway. "Have you ever heard the story of Ruth and Boaz?"

Sam uncrossed her arms and put both hands in the front pockets of her blue jeans.

"No. That from the Bible or something?"

Millie nodded. "It's kind of like the world's first Harlequin romance book. Boaz lived in Israel and Ruth was from Moab. Ruth's mother-in-law was also an Israelite but moved to Moab during a famine. Ruth married Naomi's son, but then the son died. Naomi moved back to Israel, because there was nothing there for her in Moab. Ruth loved Naomi so much, that she moved from her home in Moab, to Israel with Naomi. They were poor, so Ruth had to work all day in the fields, picking up scraps of grain so they'd have enough to eat."

Sam interrupted her. "This doesn't sound like much of a love story to me, Millie."

Millie frowned her disapproval. "Just be patient, child. I'm getting to the romantic part."

A bird flew by and she watched it until it landed in a nearby tree. Then she continued her story.

"In the same area, there was a relative of Naomi's named Boaz. He was a rich man, and he noticed Ruth working in the fields all day to gather scraps. And Ruth was a pretty good-looking woman, a real hottie in today's vernacular. So Boaz told his hired hands to leave some grain behind for Ruth to collect. Boaz was a really nice man, but I think he was getting a bit of a crush on Ruth after a few days. But most important, he wanted to do the right thing. You see, Ruth and Naomi were both widows, so they had no one to protect and care for them, and that was pretty important back then because it was a pretty rough neighborhood." She paused. "Kind of like the way things are right now."

The bird flew away and Millie watched it before going on with the story. "Back in those days it was important to carry on the family name, but if Ruth didn't remarry, then she'd have no kids and, well, you can see the problem. So the Jews set up this system called a kinsmen redeemer, where Boaz could marry her and make sure the lineage didn't end. So Naomi, who was a bit of a matchmaker, told Ruth to go and sleep at Boaz' feet near the campfire, you know, kind of to let him know she was interested and to prime the pump and that's all it took. The very next day Boaz sprang into action and took care of business."

Sam wasn't quite following her. "Sprang into action? What does that mean exactly?"

"Well, I'm getting to that part. You are so impatient, girl!" Millie brushed her long, grey hair out away from her forehead. "So Boaz went to the town elders, bought back Naomi's land and then married Ruth. And then they had babies of their own and the family name was saved."

Samantha waited for more but Millie stayed silent, just looking at her, waiting for a reaction.

"I don't get it, Millie. Why was that so important? Lots of women never get married and lots more never have kids. What's the big deal?"

Millie nodded her head patiently. "Yes, I understand why you'd feel that way, but, back then it was one of the most important things in the world. You're just going to have to trust me on this one." And then she hesitated as if a revelation had just come to her. "Sam, do you know that King David's ancestors were Ruth and Boaz?" Samantha shook her head. "And did you know that Jesus Christ was descended from King David?"

Sam pursed her lips together. "So, wait. You're telling me that if Boaz hadn't married Ruth, then Jesus Christ wouldn't have been born?"

Millie took a half-step forward and kicked the pine needles at her feet. "Well, I don't know if I'd go that far, but ... I think God would've found a way, but ... God chose Ruth and Boaz to be the ancestors of King David and Jesus Christ. Boaz saved Ruth and Naomi from terrible poverty and hardship. Because Boaz redeemed Naomi's land and married Ruth, both women became rich and ended up having children and grandchildren and happy and beautiful lives."

Sam's lips turned down into a frown. She looked over at the closest pine bough. "So are you trying to say that a woman needs a man; that she can't be happy without one?

Because if you are, then I just don't agree with you."

Millie shrugged her shoulders. "Oh, I don't know. It worked for Ruth, and it certainly worked for me."

And suddenly Sam realized she knew very little about the woman next to her. "Where is your husband now, Millie?"

"Ray died five years ago."

"Oh, I'm so sorry."

Samantha didn't know what else to say, and she felt stupid for bringing it up.

"Don't be sorry. I like talking about Ray. He was the greatest man I've ever known. He loved me more than anyone ever could. He worked every day to make me happy. We had three children together, and now I have nine grandkids." And then a faraway look came into her eyes as she spoke. "That man gave me 45 of the best years of my life. And I miss him so much." And then she laughed spontaneously. "But I gotta tell ya, girl. That man used to make me so mad!" And then she smiled. "Seems like it's always the ones we love the most that can make us the most mad."

Samantha laughed with her now and looked down at the ground. Then she reached up and plucked a few pine needles from the tree.

"So, Millie, where are your kids now?"

And then her face clouded over again. "My two oldest used to live in Seattle. They moved there to get better jobs. They had two kids each. Two boys and two girls." She paused. "I haven't heard from them since before The Day."

There was another clumsy silence. Sam wanted to say something to make her feel better, but ... she just didn't know what words would make it right. In the end, it was

Millie who smiled again and began talking.

"My youngest daughter lives here in Pigeon Creek with her wonderful husband and five children. I've been living with them for the past five years since Ray died. And I'll move back in with them once you and Matt get married. I'm looking forward to it, actually."

And that got Sam's attention. "So, why then did you come up here if you still wanted to live with your daughter and kids?"

Millie looked at her as if the question was ludicrous. "Well, my dear young one. I moved up here because you and Matt needed me. And ..." She hesitated. "Because I felt like God wanted me to, that it was the right thing to do somehow."

After that, Sam had nothing more to say. She just wanted to think. She wanted to read more about this story of Ruth and the kinsman redeemer. She wanted to understand this crazy world that Matt lived in.

"So, Millie. Tell me more about Ruth and Boaz."

Millie smiled and reached up to grab a fist-full of pine needles. "Come on inside the cabin young lady, and I'll brew you a cup of tea. Then I'll read you the whole story straight from the book."

Sam nodded and followed the old woman back inside, not believing that she was actually anxious to be read to from the Bible.

> *"I would'st not harm thee brother, but thou standest where I am about to shoot."*
>
> *– an unknown Quaker*

CHAPTER 15

Near the Oregon-Idaho Border

AS HE DROVE DOWN THE GRAVEL road, Marvin listened to the gentle sobbing of his wife as she sat beside him, her face buried in her hands. He drove another half mile before looking around to make sure there were no houses or cars, then he pulled over to the grass and shut off the engine.

"Let me check out that cut on your face, honey."

But Alexandra didn't move; she just kept crying into her own lap. Marvin tried again.

"Honey, please. I need to look at that and clean it up so it doesn't get infected on you."

But she still didn't move. Deep inside him a myriad of conflicting emotions were swirling around, each vying for dominance. Fear, anger, remorse, guilt, shame as well as relief at still being alive. He reached his right hand over and stroked her back. Her back stiffened when he touched her, but he kept his hand there, nonetheless. As softly as he could, he moved his hand in circles across her back, soothing her, trying to comfort her. He decided to say nothing, at least for now. Deep in his heart, he knew that his wife would never again be the same, because he was going through the same trauma. He hated killing people more than anything else he'd ever done. In fact, he didn't even like himself for being able to do it without hesitation.

The image flashed in his mind again. He'd stepped to the left while drawing his Glock in one fluid motion, then raised up the gun, found the front sight, placed it on the man's chest and pressed the trigger over and over again, in a rhythm that he could still hear in his mind. It was a simple process that he could repeat, a bit of work like taking out the trash or doing the dishes. And that bothered him. He would never be rid of that memory; he knew it in the very depths of his soul. Marvin had proven twice now that he could kill when he had too, but he would never enjoy it.

Marvin continued to rub her back for another fifteen minutes, all the while, glancing up at the rear-view mirror to make sure no one else was sneaking up on them. Just then he saw the red and blue strobe lights of the police car that was closing in about a half a mile behind them. A rush of fear washed over him now, and he couldn't help but wonder, *what is going to happen to us now*?

Marvin didn't stop rubbing Alexandra's back, but he caught himself thinking, *I fired 5 rounds so I've only got 10 left in my Glock. I need to reload.* But Marvin didn't do that. He knew in his heart that he could never shoot a cop, even if the officer was here to arrest them both and throw them in jail. Marvin would rather rot in jail than shoot a police officer.

So, he sat in the car and waited patiently as the cruiser pulled up behind them. There was a short blast on the siren, then the police officer's voice came over his PA system.

"Listen, folks. I know what just happened back at the Shell station. I already talked to Rob across the street and he told me everything that happened." There was a pause, then he continued. "I just need to know that both of you are safe, and that you don't need medical attention. If you could just roll your window all the way down and put both your hands outside where I can see them, well, then I'll come on up and we can talk for a bit."

Inside the Land Rover, Alex looked up, as if just now realizing what was going on. Her weeping got even louder.

"Marvin, we're going to jail! We killed a man!"

Marvin tried to reassure her as best he could as he rolled down the window on his side and hung both his hands out the window.

"It's going to be okay, Alex. Just keep your hands where he can see them and don't move real fast. I think he's a good guy."

He heard the door of the cruiser slam shut and watched in the rear-view mirror as the officer approached cautiously with his right hand on the grip of his gun.

When he reached Marvin's door, he peeked inside, saw Marvin looking down at the ground as he held his hands in plain view. He seemed to relax a little when Alexandra turned to look at him. He saw her red, puffy eyes, the look of despair, as well as the dried blood on her face. He looked at Marvin and nodded his head.

"We didn't do anything wrong, officer. They were going to kill me and steal our car."

The police officer nodded slowly. "I think I know that. It's probably a stupid question to ask, but are there any weapons inside the vehicle?"

Marvin tried to smile, but he couldn't. He just answered the question in as nonthreatening a manner as possible.

"Yeah, we got guns in here. My Glock 19 is in an appendix carry rig, and we have a carbine, a shotgun and a few other pistols, but they're all unloaded and locked up inside cases."

Just then Alex started to reach under the front seat.

"Marvin I still got this gun from the clerk. The big one."

The officer's hand went down to his pistol and he drew it in one, fluid motion. Marvin yelled at Alex to freeze, while moving between her and the cop. He raised his hands up and shoved them outside the window again. He yelled as loud as he could at his wife.

"Freeze, Alex! Don't reach for that gun!"

The cop was yelling too while pointing the pistol first at Marvin and then at Alex. Alex screamed over and over again. Finally, everyone stopped screaming, almost in unison, and the country road became deathly silent. Marvin stayed with his hands out the window, trying to look as nonthreatening as possible. A small dog barked off in the distance. Alex was the first to speak.

"I ... um, just thought you might want the gun. I guess it's evidence or something?"

The cop's arms were still locked out in front of him. In normal times, he would've already shot them both, but now ... he just didn't know what to do in a case like this. In the end, he followed his gut.

"Okay, folks. Like I said before. I know what happened. But you have to promise me not to reach for any more guns." The dog was still barking off to the west. "Are we agreed?"

Marvin nodded his head and Alex did too.

"Okay then, we'll start with the young lady." He took a step to his left. "I'd like you to very slowly get out of the car and walk up to the front and place your hands on the hood. Will you do that for me please?"

Alex nodded and got out painfully slow and did exactly as she was instructed. "Okay, great. Now don't move a muscle, Ma'am." Then the officer turned his attention back to Marvin. "Sir, I'd like you to do the same please."

Marvin got out slowly and moved to place his hands on the hood. The cop walked up behind him. "Spread your legs wider, sir."

Marvin did so. "Keep our hands on the hood, I'm just going to temporarily separate you from your gun for my own safety and give you a brief pat down. The officer holstered his pistol and reached around Marvin's right side to unholster the Glock. He then put it in the small of his own back as he checked Marvin's waist, thighs and armpits for more weapons. He then checked Alex in the same way. He noticed that Alex was crying again.

Finally satisfied that they were no immediate threat to him, he backed up three paces. "Okay, folks, you can turn around slowly and please keep your hands where I can see them while we straighten this whole thing out."

The field off to the side of the road was arid and dry, A small bird flitted out of a bush that Marvin couldn't identify. He thought it odd that he even noticed it under the circumstances.

"We'll start with you, sir. Let's see some identification."

"Yes, sir." Marvin reached back slowly for his wallet. He always carried it in his left, back pocket. He tried to hand it to the officer.

"Please take out your license and hand it to me, please."

Marvin did so, and the cop looked down at it. Then back up at Marvin. A confused look came over his face. "You're Marvin Tubbs?"

"Yes, sir."

The cop smiled slightly.

"Marvin Tubbs of *The Mad American Show*?"

Marvin tilted his lead to one side and nodded.

"That's right."

The cop gestured with his head over to Alex. "And this is your beautiful wife?"

Marvin nodded again. The cop's smile got even bigger. "Do you have a business card in your wallet to verify that?"

"Yeah, sure." Marvin reached into his wallet and handed the officer his card. The officer looked at it and started to laugh out loud.

"Well I'll be snookered." And then he glanced back to his police cruiser. "Listen, just wait here. Don't move a muscle. I've got to get something from my car." He turned to leave and glanced back at them both. "Don't move now." They both nodded in agreement.

After he left, Marvin looked over at Alex and their eyes met. "Is he going to kill us, Marv?" But Marvin said nothing. The cop came back holding something in his left hand.

"Mr. Tubbs, would you be so kind as to sign this copy of your book? It would mean the world to me."

Marvin looked over at Alex and then back at the police officer. "Well, I guess I'd better or else you might shoot me."

The cop laughed and stepped forward. He slapped Marvin's left shoulder and handed him the book. It was a worn copy of *The Mad American Comes Unglued*. The policeman reached into his left, breast pocket and handed Marvin an ink pen.

"Mr. Tubbs, I could never shoot you. I listen to your show every day while I'm out on patrol. It helps break the monotony of the job. Things aren't usually all that exciting here in the little town of Buster Gulch."

Marvin placed the book on the hood of his Land Rover and opened to the first page. "Who shall I make it out to?"

"Make it out to Glen and Sasha if you would. Sasha's my wife, and she's a fan too."

Marvin nodded and signed the book before handing it back to him. He glanced over at Alex who was still bending over the Land Rover with her hands on the hood.

"Do you mind if my wife moves now?"

Glen laughed out loud and waved with his hands. "Ah, sure, no problem at all." And then he reached back to get Marvin's Glock. He looked at it briefly and then handed it back to Marvin, being careful to keep the muzzle pointed in a safe direction. Marvin accepted it with hesitation before placing it back in its holster.

When Marvin looked up, Alex was turned around, her face still white as a sheet. The cop was smiling from ear to ear.

"Wow! I touched Marvin Tubb's Glock. That is just incredible." And then he seemed to come back down to earth and regain his professional bearing.

"Hey, folks, I'm sorry I had to draw down on you like that, I just thought your wife was going for a gun is all."

Marvin nodded. "We understand, don't we, honey."

Alex nodded but said nothing.

"Mrs. Tubbs, you were right about the 44 magnum revolver. I'm gonna need that. Not so much for evidence, but simply because it doesn't belong to you." He hesitated. "Al, the station clerk, he's dead and I'll give that to his wife. It belongs to her now." And then his face clouded over.

"Al was a good man. Known him my whole life." And then he looked Alex in the eyes. "I'm glad you shot his killer, ma'am." The little dog in the distance started barking again. "One shot between the eyes. "Helluva shot, Ma'am." And then he looked over at Marvin. "I counted five holes in the other guy. "Good shooting, both of you."

And then a clumsiness seemed to set in among the trio. For several seconds no one moved or said anything. Alexandra leaned against the Land Rover and suddenly went down on the ground in a heap. Marvin moved to catch her and managed to keep her from hitting her head on the bumper or the gravel road. Glen moved in to help him as well. They laid her down on the brown grass beside the road. The cop spoke first. "I think she's in shock. Raise up her feet about 10 inches." Marvin complied, and the color in Alexandra's face seemed to return.

"She just shot a man. It's been a rough day, Glen."

The officer nodded. "Yeah, I can imagine."

Alex opened her eyes.

"It's okay, baby. Everything's fine."

After a few minutes she was able to sit up on her own with her back to the bumper of the Land Rover.

"I feel very weak." She held her head in her hands.

Marvin gave her a hug. "It's okay, honey. You did great today. You saved my life."

"You okay, now, ma'am?"

Alex nodded gently.

"Well, okay then. Let me get that 44 out of your car, then you can both follow me back into town."

Marvin called after him with a worried voice. "Are we under arrest then?"

Officer Glen laughed again. "No way, man! I'm taking you to my house so my wife can meet you."

A weak smile came over Alex as she realized for the first time that she wasn't going to prison. Marvin helped her get up. She was shaky at first, but Marvin managed to get her inside the car.

Once the officer was inside his cruiser, he turned off the strobe lights and turned his car around. He talked to himself inside the cruiser.

"Wow! I can't believe this! The Mad American right here in Buster Gulch!" He shook his head from side to side, then looked in the rear-view mirror to make sure he was being followed. "Sasha is not going to believe this!"

"The enemy will never attack you where you are strongest. . . . He will attack where you are weakest. If you do not know your weakest point, be certain, your enemy will."

– William R. Forstchen, One Second After

CHAPTER 16

Off the Oregon Coastline

MAJOR CHAO LOOKED TO THE east and saw the emerald coast before him with the coastal mountains behind it. They'd seen very few other ships on the trans-Pacific voyage, but now they were seeing a few small fishing boats off the coast. He went to the wheelhouse again and spent an hour monitoring radio traffic. He picked up some short wave intel but it was all local and all civilian. From what he could decipher using his limited English, there was still a functioning federal government, and the United States military was still very much a threat. That discovery pushed away his earlier doubts about his mission, and he determined himself to carry out his orders without question. He tried one last time to radio Beijing, but with no luck.

While his men used the boom to lift the large crate out

of the fish hold and place it on the deck, Chao knew that he'd crossed the line of no return. He watched as the nuclear engineers supervised the unpacking of the crate, and then the final assembly. It took them most of the morning and afternoon to prepare the missile for final launch.

As he looked on, one of his men walked up and saluted him crisply. The major returned his salute.

"Yes, what is it?"

The younger man seemed a bit nervous as he asked his question.

"Well, sir, the other men are wondering what we'll do after the launch?"

Major Chao pondered the man's question a moment before responding. The major knew something very important that his men did not. This had never been a two-way mission. Upon launch, the exhaust of the big rocket would likely set the fishing trawler on fire. It might sink, or it might not; no one really knew for sure. He suspected that both nuclear engineers had also surmised this as well, since they were now wearing life jackets. Major Chao didn't directly answer his question.

"Assemble the men aft."

The soldier nodded, saluted and then stepped back before doing a perfect about-face. Five minutes later, Chao was standing before his five men as well as the captain of the ship and his crew.

"We are almost ready to launch. This is a large rocket. Too large to be launched off the deck of this boat without causing damage." He paused. "How much damage, we don't yet know." Forward the ship, Chao could hear the engineers talking in hushed tones. "One of two things will happen. Either the ship will sink or we'll be able to repair the damage and sail back to our homeland."

The nine men before him looked around nervously; they were afraid to ask the obvious question, so Chao did it for them.

"If the ship sinks, then we'll take the small boats ashore. Then we'll travel to the city of Newport, where a United States Coast Guard vessel is anchored. We'll take the ship and use it to sail back to China."

Several of the men smiled, but the rest still looked apprehensive. He did his best to look confident, but it was difficult, since he didn't know if any of his story was true. He just knew that the men needed hope; they needed to know that there was a chance they could make it back home. Whether or not his story was true didn't matter. He'd given them enough hope to cooperate with finishing the mission, and that's all that mattered.

"Go now and prepare the life boats for casting off, just in case. Also prepare for damage control. We'll need fire extinguishers, and water buckets."

He saluted and dismissed the men. They scurried off with newfound purpose, convinced that their only chance of survival was to carry out his orders.

Three hours later, the missile was ready to launch. It stood almost as tall as the ship was long, and it rocked precariously on the tiny swells. Fortunately, the weather was mild today or it might have slid off the deck and into the ocean. Chao was an atheist, or he would have prayed for safety.

When all the men were aft the ship, as far away as they could get from the rocket, the engineers initiated the launch sequence. The engineers knew what was about to happen, so they' wisely rushed to the back of the ship with the others.

Major Chao watched the numbers count down on the

digital read-out held by the Lead Engineer.

Five, four, three, two, one.

At first there was nothing, but then a deafening noise issued from the back of the rocket. Chao looked over and saw both engineers jump into the ocean. As the sound increased, flames built up intensity and shot out the back of the rocket, using the ship itself as a blast plate.

The rocket rose slowly at first, but then quickly gained speed. Major Chao stood transfixed at the sight of the flames that quickly engulfed the ship. And that's when he realized that he'd been purposely sent on a suicide mission. He would never see his family again, even if they were still alive.

Several of his men jumped off into the ocean, but Chao clicked his heels together in the position of attention, as the growing flames seared his sight and ripped the flesh away from his body. He was dead in two seconds.

The rocket was away now, and the boat broke in half and sank quickly into the ocean. One of the engineers had survived, and he looked on now, bobbing up and down in the water, as the rocket raced upward into the Stratosphere. The missile wouldn't be accurate, but he knew that it didn't need to be.

Mountain Home Air Force Base

PRESIDENT ROGER THORNTON WAS IN A MEETING when the secret service agent rushed into the conference room and grabbed him by the arm.

"Hurry, sir, we have an inbound missile off the West Coast. We need to get you underground, sir."

Roger didn't hesitate or argue. He'd been briefed on the possibility of this happening, so he just held on to the arms of his wheelchair as the agent pushed him out of the room and into an elevator. Chairman of the Joint Chiefs, General Ashby was quickly by his side as the elevator doors closed and they started to move down.

"Someone tell me what's going on!"

Agent Delgado answered him briskly. "A single missile launch off the coast of Oregon. We don't know the destination. Just that it's headed east somewhere into the continental US."

Roger looked over at General Ashby for more information. The four-star general shrugged his shoulders helplessly. "I need to get in touch with the CIC if we want real-time information."

"So what's your best guess?"

The general looked amazingly calm for the situation, and that bothered Roger for some reason.

"I see two options. Either it's an EMP strike or somehow one of our enemies figured out you're here and ..."

Just then the elevator lurched to a stop and the lights went completely dark. It was a second or two before the emergency lighting kicked in. Agent Delgado moved forward in the dimness and began pressing elevator buttons, but nothing seemed to work. He pressed the transmitter on his comms gear before speaking. "This is Mustang. Give me a sit-rep, please."

There was no answer, so he tried again. "This is Mustang. I'm trapped with the president in the conference room elevator. We need help."

Agent Delgado looked at the president and shook his head from side to side.

"Nothing, Mr. President."

Roger looked over at the general expectantly, but no answer was immediately forthcoming. Roger's heart sank. The general finally spoke.

"EMP strike."

Roger let his head drop down until his chin rested on his chest. When he spoke again, it was with a desperate fervor.

"Lord, God help us."

Buster Gulch, Oregon

Marvin and Alexandra waved and smiled as they pulled away from Glen's home in Buster Gulch. The police officer and his wife, Sasha, were standing in the driveway waving as they pulled out onto the main road again.

Marvin had wanted to get on the road as quickly as possible, but he could tell that Alex needed to stay, that she needed time to recover from shooting a man, and Glen, the police officer, along with his wife were very good therapy for her. After a late lunch of meat loaf and baked potatoes, Sasha and Alex had talked for two hours. Marv had spoken with Glen as well, but mostly had picked Glen's brain for any information that might help them make it safely back to Pigeon Creek.

Glen had even called ahead to the next county just to make sure there was no trouble on their route into Idaho. And now, for the third time on their journey, they'd accepted help from strangers, first from an old man named Harold, then from a retired Marine Corps sergeant major, and now from a police officer and his wife.

Alex was quiet until they got about a mile out of town, before finally breaking the silence.

"Those were nice people."

Marvin nodded his head.

"Yes they were."

Alex looked out the window and watched the arid landscape flash by as they drove.

"I needed that Marv."

Marvin didn't say anything.

"I need nice people in my life. Civilized people. Not those crazy ones that make me shoot them."

Again, Marvin said nothing.

"I guess I just needed to be reminded that even though the world's gone nuts that there's still people out there like you and me who still care about strangers."

Marvin thought about that for a few seconds before answering. Finally, he sighed and nodded his head.

"I know what you mean, babe. It's like these hard times are bringing out the best and worst of what's inside people. Folks are either getting better or worse, and it's forcing people to choose sides."

Alexandra turned sideways to look at him. "So how do we know who to trust and who to shoot? It all happens so fast that it overwhelms me."

Marvin gripped the steering wheel tighter. He'd been thinking the same thing, wondering, who to trust and who not to trust.

"Guess we need to stay sharp and just trust our instincts." He paused. "And each other."

Alex agreed silently by nodding her head. And then she reached into the back seat and started digging around for something inside a bag.

"What are you looking for?"

But she didn't answer him. When she turned back around in her seat, she was holding a pair of scissors in her right hand.

"What's that for?"

Alex hung her head down and started cutting away at the long beautiful locks of her brunette hair. She didn't stop until a large pile of hair was lying on the floor of the Land Rover. At first, Marv didn't say anything, He knew what she was doing and why she was doing it, and it made him angry that his wife was forced to do this just to survive. But he knew it was the right thing to do, so he encouraged her as best he could.

"That looks nice, sweetheart."

Alex didn't say anything. She knew it didn't look nice, and that was the whole point. She flipped the visor down and looked closely into the mirror before cutting a bit more to even things out. Then she took some wet wipes out of the door pocket and began cleaning off her make-up. When she was done, she turned over toward Marvin,

"Okay, sweetheart, am I ugly enough now?"

Marvin slowed the car and forced a smile onto his lips. They had just left the Oregon state line behind them. "If I had a dog as ugly as you, I'd shave his ..."

But Marv never finished the sentence. Suddenly, without any warning whatsoever, the engine on the Land Rover turned itself off. He looked down at the steering wheel perplexed.

"What is going on, Marvin?"

The power steering was out, so Marvin manhandled the steering wheel as the car slowed to a stop on the side of the road. Marvin tried to restart the car, but it was useless. They had zero power. He popped the hood and opened up his door before getting out and opening up the engine compartment. He looked down at all the engine parts and was at a loss as to what to do.

Alex got out and was standing beside him now. "What is it, Marv?"

He sighed helplessly. "I have no idea, Alex. It was running great and then it just stopped. It's not overheated or anything. It all looks fine. The gauges were all normal."

And then a thought came to him. "Where's your cell phone, honey?"

She pulled it out of the back pocket of her jeans. "I doubt we have any service though. It's been a long time."

She looked at her phone and then frowned. "It's dead, Marv." She looked over at him with a confused look on her face. "Marv I just checked it before we left Buster Gulch. It was all charged up."

Marvin pulled out his own cell phone and showed her the black screen. He reached up and closed the hood with a slam.

He glanced to his left at a cell phone tower off in the distance. He watched it closely for several seconds.

"There's no blinking light on top of that tower." He went inside the Land Rover again and rummaged through his gear. Alex followed him. He picked up the two-way radio that Matt had given him and turned it on.

Nothing. No power anywhere.

And then it occurred to him. He looked up into the sky and into the fading sunlight. Then he looked over at Alex. He stared into her blue eyes.

"It's an EMP, honey."

"What does that mean?"

Marvin leaned up against the Land Rover.

"It means that I love you. But it also means that we'll be walking all the way back to Pigeon Creek."

You, Lord, are my lamp; the Lord turns my darkness into light.

2 Samuel 22:29 (NIV)

CHAPTER 17

SAMANTHA VANDERVEEN AND Matthew Robbins were married on a beautiful Indian Summer day inside the old, white Bible church on the outskirts of Pigeon Creek. Samantha had been dreaming about this day for most of her life, but it was nothing close to any of her dreams. Instead of hiring an elite and expensive wedding planner, it was cobbled together at the last minute by the Pigeon Creek Bible Church Ladies Auxiliary. The cake wasn't professionally made and 5 layers high, and it didn't cost 3,000 dollars like she'd envisioned, but was a single-layer sheet cake made by Theresa Gibbons at the diner out of a Betty crocker box mix. All she did was add an egg and some water before baking. Instead of decorating with a thousand roses, Matt wanted to use pine boughs. And since there were very few flowers available this time of year in the mountains, Samantha had acquiesced.

Her wedding gown wasn't even hers. It belonged to Theresa who'd graciously loaned it to her. Matt didn't wear a tuxedo, because he didn't own one, and the nearest formal attire rental store was in Boise and probably looted and closed down for the next thousand years or so. Instead of a white, stretched limousine, the new couple drove back to Matt;s cabin in his Dodge Ram pick-up truck.

The reception, which normally would've cost well into the 5-figure range was a pot-luck dinner put on by the church. Matt had to explain to her exactly what a pot-luck dinner was, and the initial thought of eating other people's food had appalled her, but ... in the end it had been just fine, although there were several of the hot dishes she'd passed on, simply because no one could identify the type of meat inside the pot.

But by far the saddest part was the absence of her parents and her sister, Alexandra. But none of that could be helped, and she knew that. For all she knew, every last person she knew and loved was already dead, save her new husband. Nonetheless, deep inside she still harbored the hope that Alex and Marvin would arrive at any minute to help her celebrate her wedding day. But they never showed.

It was still four in the afternoon when everyone left the church, and the newlyweds pulled into Matt's driveway. Matt turned off the engine and looked over at Samantha. He was saddened to see tears running down her cheeks. Matt didn't know what to say, so he stayed quiet for several seconds. Then he unbuckled his seat belt and dropped his head down onto her own. She leaned into him as well.

"I'm sorry, Samantha. I know this isn't the wedding

you've always dreamed of."

Samantha reached over with her right hand and pushed aside his sport coat and placed it on his chest. She was still crying, but she was also smiling, and that confused Matt.

"Honey, you're smiling and crying simultaneously, and I don't know what to think about that."

She didn't answer him directly. Instead, she answered his statement with a question. "Are you happy, Matt?"

Matt immediately smiled, and then he put his arms around her and hugged his new bride as tight as he dared. " I am very happy, Samantha." He hesitated, a little afraid to follow up with the obvious question. "But are you happy, Sam?"

The woman in his arms was quiet for a moment, and that made Matt even more nervous. Finally, she answered him directly. "Matt, I've been a selfish woman my whole life. Always arranging my life so that everything benefitted me regardless of how it affected others, but ..." Her voice tapered off into nothing. Matt prompted her.

"But what? Tell me."

She sighed audibly. "I don't want to be that person anymore, Matt. Life isn't about just me. It's about the people around me." She paused but Matt didn't respond, so she went on. "Life is about you. It's about Theresa and Luke and their little girl, Lacey. It's even about the pastor and Millie who are very nice but need to mind their own business."

Matt smiled. "Sorry, honey. I hope they didn't pressure you into marrying me?"

Sam wiped a tear from her silver-blue eyes and laughed out loud. Then she lifted her head and looked her husband directly in the eyes. "No, honey. They didn't pressure me.

I married you because I'm madly in love with you and I would've married you despite the circumstances. But I gotta admit that the apocalypse may have sped up the process."

Matt lowered his head down to her face and placed his lips on her own. Samantha responded emotionally and physically to his kisses as she pulled him down onto the seat of the truck. For five minutes they didn't talk. Then, suddenly and without warning, Samantha blurted out, "Take me inside, Matt. I want to have a baby."

In the throes of heated passion Matt didn't argue with her. "Whatever makes you happy, honey." He clumsily reached behind him to open the truck door, then, as she held onto his neck with both hands, he picked her up and carried her into the cabin to begin their honeymoon.

Pigeon Creek Diner

THERESA AND LUKE GIBBONS WERE INSIDE THE Pigeon Creek Diner after the wedding and reception. Luke was at his favorite table beside his 3-year-old daughter, Lacy. She crawled up onto his lap and colored quietly while Theresa walked up with a cup of coffee for her husband.

"That was such a beautiful wedding, wasn't it, honey?" Luke was deep in thought, but nodded his head and grunted softly out loud. She sat down at the booth across from her husband and daughter. She just smiled at them both, and didn't say anything more at first. She knew that Luke was deep in thought, and that when he was ready to talk, then he'd let out with it, but not a moment before. Theresa turned her attention to Lacy.

"What ya drawing, sweetie?"

The little girl didn't look up. She just kept drawing as she talked. "It's Daddy shooting bad guys."

That statement got Luke's attention. He pulled himself out of his deep contemplation and looked down at the drawing of stick people on the white napkin in front of his daughter. There were two dead stick people on the ground and Luke was standing over them with his pistol pointing down. There was a big star pinned on his stick chest.

He looked up and over at his wife. A frown spread across his face, but he didn't say anything. Neither did Theresa. They both just watched as the little girl colored the stick figures. The dinner crowd had already left. There were fewer and fewer customers with each passing day, and Theresa hadn't gotten a grocery shipment since the bombs started to fall. She was almost out of supplies, so they'd have to close down soon.

She stood up and moved over beside Lacy. "Let's go girl. Time for your nap." The little girl didn't resist and Theresa took her to the back room and lay her daughter down onto the foam mattress that was reserved for just this occasion. A few minutes later she was back out sitting beside Luke. He spoke first.

"Didn't you tell me she's been having nightmares lately?

Theresa nodded her head. "Yeah. Ever since that shoot-out down at the grocery store." She hesitated a moment. "You seem to be sleeping okay though."

Luke reached across the table top and took her hand in his, resting it atop the red Formica. "Yeah. I'm okay. I think about it during the day quite a bit, though."

She pressed him further. "And?"

He shrugged his shoulders just a tad. "And ... I don't know how to process it." He picked his coffee mug up with his free hand and blew away the steam before taking a tiny sip. "I never really thought I'd have to shoot anyone, not here in Pigeon Creek anyways. It's not something I expected to have to deal with."

Theresa nodded her head sympathetically. "I understand. I didn't see it coming either. She squeezed his hand reassuringly. "But then ... I didn't see economic collapse and a nuclear war coming down the pike either."

She waited for him to respond, but his mouth didn't open. Finally, she leaned her head in closer to his from across the table. "You did what you had to do, Luke. You did what any decent cop would've done. You saw bad guys killing good guys so you followed your training and had to shoot some people. It's as simple as that."

Luke placed his left hand atop his coffee mug and felt the warmth rise up and hit the palm of his hand. "Matt had to kill as well, but he doesn't seem to have any problem with it." He paused and then glanced at the window and up the mountain. "He's up at his cabin right now on his honeymoon. I don't think it bothers him at all." He took a sip of his coffee. "I don't get it, Theresa. Why would it bother me and not him? I'm a cop for heaven's sake. I'm supposed to be able to deal with this."

His wife smiled at him softly. "Well, honey. First off, I don't think you should assume that it isn't bothering Matt, because it is."

Luke looked up and over at her. "How do you know that?"

"Because Matt shared it with Sam and she shared it with me."

Luke suddenly looked down and laughed just a tiny bit. "You women. You're always talking to each other. Why do you do that?"

She looked out the big picture window to her right at the sun. It was getting lower in the sky now. "I don't know, Luke. Why don't you men talk more to each other? I think it's stupid that you all stuff your feelings down inside and never let them see the light of day." She paused. "It's not healthy, Luke."

Luke sipped his coffee again. "Well, that may be so, but I think women talk too much about their feelings."

Theresa raised her eyebrows up at him. "Oh really? Well, I think men talk too little about their emotions."

Luke didn't say anything in return. He just turned his head into the sunset and watched the yellow orb sink painfully down toward the horizon. Theresa waited for over a minute, secretly praying that he would talk to her, but ... his lips were sealed. Finally, she broke down and spoke.

"Maybe you should ask Matt if it's bothering him. You don't have to admit that it's bothering you too, but he's a civilian, and he might appreciate getting it out in the open, You might be able to help him get through it."

Luke thought about it for several seconds, then slowly turned his face back to his wife. He leaned his head forward over the table. "I see what you're doing Theresa Lynn."

She smiled. "And?"

"Kiss me quick, woman."

Theresa leaned forward and kissed her husband on the lips. He smiled, so she kissed him again, this time with more passion.

"I suppose, maybe ... maybe I could mention it to him." He leaned back in the bench seat and raised up his coffee much. "You know. As a favor to my friend just in case he needs to talk about it."

Theresa let his other hand go free and he moved both

his hands down to encircle his coffee mug. She looked briefly out into the setting sun, and then quickly back over to Luke and met his gaze. A serious look came over her face.

"You're a good and decent man Luke Gibbons." She paused before finishing. "And I love you for it."

Luke met her gaze and held it as long as he could before having to look away. He always had trouble holding her gaze, not because of any feelings of shame, but simply because he knew in his heart that she was a better person than he was, and just being around her made him a better man. He thought about it silently for a few seconds, and he wondered to himself, *Does she even know how much I appreciate her and how much I love her? Does she know that I'd be lost without her?* But he wiped the silly thought out of his mind. Of course she does. And he vowed not to think silly thoughts like that ever again.

But what Luke didn't realize was that Theresa wanted him more than anything to share his feelings with her. Not just wanted it ... she needed it. Unfortunately, like most men, thoughts like that were oblivious to Luke. Talking about his feelings was a sign of weakness, and he needed to remain strong for her and Lacy, especially during the apocalypse when everything around them was falling apart. No, he would be strong. He would hold it all together and keep soldiering on, because he loved his family. Fortunately for him, Theresa understood men more than he understood women.

The heat in his coffee mug was gone now, and Theresa, as if reading his thoughts, reached over and took it from his hands.

"Let me nuke that for you honey."

She got up and walked over behind the counter and

placed the cup in the microwave. She punched in 30 seconds and waited. Fifteen seconds passed and the microwave stopped. But not just that, all the lights in the diner went dark as well. Theresa glanced over at him

"Honey, will you do your man magic and go reset the breaker switch?"

But Luke didn't move to accommodate her request. Instead, he stood up and pressed his face closer to the window. "Theresa, come here?"

Slightly alarmed, his wife forgot about the microwave and walked over to him. She looked out the window as well. "What's wrong, honey?"

Luke nodded at the coming darkness. "The streetlights should be coming on, but they're not." He looked over at her. "I think this is a power outage."

And then he pulled the radio mike off his tactical vest and keyed it, but there was no sound. Theresa pulled out her cell phone from her apron and pressed the home screen. Then she pressed a few other buttons. She looked up at him, with desperation and a bit of fear in her eyes.

"It's dead, Luke. Not even a light."

Luke pulled out his own cell phone, but it was dead as well. He looked over at her, out at the sunset, then back to his wife again. He let out a tired sigh. "Let's get Lacy and head home. There's nothing more we can do here."

Theresa got their daughter and they locked up the darkened diner and hopped into the police SUV. Luke pressed the ignition button, but nothing happened. Only then did the full extent of what had happened begin to set in. They looked at each other in the coming darkness, neither knowing what to say.

"The mountains are calling, and I must go."

– John Muir

CHAPTER 18

<u>*10 miles inside Idaho*</u>

"**W**ELL, AT LEAST WE MADE it to Idaho." Alex looked over to her husband and frowned before answering him.

"Is that supposed to make me feel better, Marvin. Really?"

He pasted on a fake smile. "Just trying to look on the bright side, honey." She didn't answer him, so he leaned his butt up against the side of the Land Rover. It had been 30 minutes since the vehicle had stopped, and he had no idea what he should do. They were stranded, and, if this really was an EMP, then this shiny, new motorized vehicle, jam-packed with computer chips and circuitry, would never run again. He glanced back at all the equipment inside, stacked to the ceiling. He shook his head from side to side.

"We have to walk the rest of the way, Alex."

Alexandra's eyes narrowed, and her face took on a look that didn't understand what he'd just said. All she could do was repeat his statement, as if trying to come to grips with this new reality. "We have to walk the rest of the way?"

Marve nodded. "Yep."

She looked at the fields on both sides of the road. There were about 10 cows looking at her from behind a barbed wire fence on the left side of he road, chewing their cuds, totally oblivious to the electromagnetic pulse and the severity of what had just happened. They seemed to be mocking her.

"How far is it to Pigeon Creek?"

Marve looked at the mountains far off to the north and south of him. They seemed to be miles away, but he didn't know how far off they were. He tried to sound positive when he answered his wife.

"Oh, I don't know exactly. About ... say ... less than a hundred miles."

Alexandra's response was less positive. "A hundred miles! Are you out of your mind! We can't walk a hundred miles!"

She was staring right at him now, but Marvin didn't meet her gaze. "No, I said *less* than a hundred miles."

She shook her head from side to side before placing her head down onto the hood of the Land Rover and crying in despair. "I can't do it, Marvin. This is too much."

Marve moved to the other side of the Land Rover and tried to hold her, but she pushed him away. "Get away from me, Marvin Tubbs. This is all your fault!"

Marve took a step back and placed his hand on his left chin in contemplative thought. *How is this my fault?* But he didn't dare say the question out loud. He was quiet for a full minute as she sobbed on the hood of the Rover. In the end, he decided to just be quiet for a while, and to try and think things through rationally and calmly.

A few minutes later, he knew they'd have to leave the Land Rover and most of their belongings. In his mind he started to make a checklist of what they'd need to complete the 100-mile hike. Then he walked around his wife to the other side of the Land Rover. He opened the back door and looked inside. Alex spoke to him through tiny sobs.

"What are you doing?"

But Marve didn't answer. He reached into the back and pulled out the two backpacks and threw them onto the side of the road. He wanted to travel light, but still have what they'd need to get them all the way to Pigeon Creek.

He heard his wife's voice again, this time not crying. "What are you doing, Marve?"

He didn't look over at her when he answered, but instead kept working, moving things around, throwing things out onto the shoulder of the road.

"I have to decide what to take and what to leave."

But Alex just shook her head from side to side. "We can't leave anything behind, Marvin. This is our stuff. We have to take it all." But Marvin didn't answer her. "We can't leave our stuff here, Marvin. People will steal it." Marvin still didn't answer her. He just kept moving things around as if looking for specific items. "You're just going to have to fix the car so we can drive the rest of the way to Pigeon Creek." She folded her hands across her chest defiantly. "I refuse to walk, Marvin, when we have a perfectly good Land Rover right here in front of us. So just hurry up and get it running so we can get started."

Then Marvin saw the footlocker that Sergeant Major Stafford had placed in the back seat. He hadn't looked inside it yet. He walked around to the other side of the Rover and pulled it out with both hands. It was extremely heavy for its size. Once on the ground he unlatched it and raised the lid. He smiled when he looked inside. It was filled with military supplies from the sergeant major's basement.

On top were several claymore mines. He pulled them out and placed them carefully on the ground. Then he pulled out two sets of body armor. They were desert camo, very heavy, military grade complete with steel plates. He wondered how the old man had even carried the box up from the basement. He put them on the ground beside the claymores.

He looked up and saw that Alex had moved over and was standing next to him now. "What are those things, Marve?"

"Those are Claymore mines and body armor."

Alex' curiosity had gotten the better or her grief, so she knelt down and examined them closer. "What do they do?"

Marvin smiled. "The Claymores blow up and send buckshot into anything in front of them."

A playful smile touched her lips. "Can I touch them?" Marvin smiled as well. Then he bent down and picked one up and handed it to her. "Sure, they're harmless until we set them up and activate them. They have a kill zone of over 50 yards."

Alex ran her finger tips over the olive drab plastic face and read the words "FRONT TOWARD ENEMY". The tears were drying on her cheeks now. She handed it back to her husband. "Maybe we should take these with us,

Marvin?"

Marve didn't totally understand his wife, but he was smart enough to accept her curiosity as a gift from God. He continued unpacking the footlocker and laying items onto the ground. Marvin smiled when he saw the small box labeled "M67 Grenades." He placed them on the ground before talking to his wife. "Better not touch this box, honey. At least not until I show you how to use them."

Alex had suddenly lost all pretext of crying and was now fully absorbed in the military armaments before her. To Marvin, she looked like a 10-year-old on Christmas morning opening her presents.

"What's that thing?"

Marvin lifted out the olive-drab tube and placed it on the ground beside them. "That's the M72 LAW."

She looked perplexed. "What's it do?"

"It's a portable, one-shot anti-tank weapon. I've shot them before in training. They're fun."

Her eyes lit up. "Really? Can I shoot it?"

Marvin looked back down at the footlocker. "Let's wait and see on that one. My hope is that we never need to use any of this."

Marvin reached down and picked up one of the Ka-bar fighting knives inside its sheath and held it up to show her. She reached out and took it quickly. Then pulled it out of the sheath and started waving it around. Marvin backed up a few inches.

"Careful, honey. That thing's dangerous."

She smiled and put it back into the sheath. "Can I have this one?"

Marvin returned her smile. "Absolutely. I think it's a good pick for you. I'll show you some knife-fighting tricks when we get time."

Marvin sorted through the rest of the equipment and decided what to take and what to leave behind. He was surprised with his wife's disappointment at leaving behind the grenades, the LAW, the Claymores and the body armor. He found himself defending his decision.

"I'm sorry, honey, but it's just all so heavy and we've got to march almost a hundred miles. If we need anti-tank rockets and Claymore mines then I doubt we'll even make it back." He paused. "We'll just pack most of this stuff back up and I'll bury it off the road. As soon as we get a chance, we'll come back and get it, along with our other things, provided they're still here."

Alex nodded her head, but some of her enthusiasm had faded. "I suppose. This stuff is cool, but I don't think we can carry it all the way back." She smiled again. "I'll help you bury it."

Marvin was surprised by her change of attitude, but welcomed it nonetheless. He picked up the entrenching tool and handed it to his wife. Then he started to drag the footlocker off the road and into the field. About 20 yards in he stopped and they both took turns digging a hole about 3 feet deep. An hour later the footlocker was secure and they returned to the Land Rover to pack up before leaving.

He dug out some hiking shoes for both of them, along with tactical pants and long-sleeved shirts. He loaded up 10 magazines of 5.56 mm rounds, then he showed Alex how to operate the carbine. It was a lightweight, DPMS Panther, and she seemed to handle it well. He placed a tin can out 50 yards in the field and then taught her the basics of aiming and firing. The cows on the other side of the road got spooked and ran off the other way. She didn't hit the can, but she was able to come close. They had plenty of ammo that they had to leave behind, so he let her practice for half an hour, then he took a few practice shots of his own.

By time they'd finished and were ready to go, the sun was almost down on the horizon.

"Honey, we may as well camp here for the night and get an early start in the morning. We've got a long ways to go. Let's build a fire and cook some food. We may not get a hot meal for a while."

Alex nodded. "How long do you think it'll take us to get to Pigeon creek?"

They both gathered some dry sticks for the fire as they talked. "Probably about 10 days?"

Alex reached down to pick up a stick. "That long? Are you sure we can't move faster?"

"Sorry, honey, but that's 10 miles a day and we don't really know what we're gonna run into. It could take even longer than that if there's trouble."

Alex frowned. "A hundred miles by Land Rover would take just a few hours." She reached down to pick up another stick. "If I hadn't talked so long to Glen's wife we could've been in Pigeon Creek before the EMP hit."

The same thought had crossed Marvin's mind, but he didn't want to hurt her feelings, so he downplayed it. "Maybe yes. Maybe no. A hundred different things could've happened to slow us down. So let's not cry over spilt milk."

Both their arms were full now, so they headed back to the Land Rover. Marve built the fire while Alex opened several cans of beef stew. When the fire had burned down to coals, they put the cans on the fire and talked as it heated.

"Thanks Marvin."

He looked confused.

"What for?"

"For putting up with me."

He smiled and glanced over at the mountain far to the north. "We're a team, babe, and a team sticks together through thick and thin."

He moved closer to her and hugged her with both arms. "I love you, Alex. You know that. I always have and I always will. Nothing will keep me away from you."

The wind picked up and smoke suddenly blew into their faces. "I love you too, babe. Sorry to be such a baby sometimes. I ..." She hesitated as they moved a few feet to the left to get out of the way of the campfire smoke.

"I don't know why I'm not as tough as you are. Sometimes I just have to cry."

He squeezed her shoulder a bit and then they took off the cans of stew and began to eat. They supplemented the stew with a loaf of stale bread, and both ate until they could eat no more.

Afterwards, they sat by the fire and stared into the red-hot coals. Alex was the first to speak. "Do you think Sam and Matt are okay?"

Marvin nodded. "Yeah, I do. From their last messages it sounds like things are getting rough there, but they're rising to the occasion and taking care of business."

She was quiet for a few seconds, but then surprised him with a confession. "I'm glad you were in the Marines, honey. I used to think it was stupid, that you made too much out of it, but ..." She moved in closer to him to share body warmth. "But now I can see how important it is."

Marvin kissed the top of her brunette head. "Chivalry is not dead."

She laughed for the first time since leaving Buster Gulch. "If it wasn't for you I'd already be dead. I would've stayed in Seattle without you. Those men on the highway would've killed me for sure, after ..."

She let the words trail off into the darkness before looking back down into the hot coals. Marvin didn't respond. He just let it go. Then he got up and pulled her to his feet. They rolled out their sleeping bags beside the fire and climbed down inside. Marvin thought about setting up a watch schedule to guard against intruders, but the truth was he was totally exhausted. They'd need a good night's sleep if they were going to be walking back to Pigeon Creek.

Marvin tried to stay awake for a few hours. Alex fell asleep first, her arm laying across his shoulder, and Marvin's hand was on her head when he finally dozed off to sleep.

They fell into deep slumber, blessed with happy dreams of life before the apocalypse. Marvin was in front of the microphone doing the Mad American Show, and Alex was having coffee with her friends in Seattle at an outrageously expensive coffee shop.

Neither of them heard the horses approach. They didn't hear the men dismount and walk up to the fire. Marvin didn't stir when the baseball bat came down on his head. In fact, he never felt a thing.

Fame is only good for one thing - they will cash your check in a small town.

– Truman Capote

CHAPTER 19

__Lights out +1__

"**S**O EXACTLY HOW LONG ARE WE GO-
ing to be without power?"

Matt had been answering their questions for the last 15 minutes, but the people of Pigeon Creek still didn't get it, so he decided to be very blunt.

"Probably for the rest of your life."

Suddenly the room was filled with silence. They were at the town hall, and all the shades were open to let in the light from the sun. It was the day after Matt's wedding, and his new bride, Samantha, was sitting off to his left listening. It was obvious that the people of Pigeon Creek were scared.

The man who'd asked the question cocked his head to the left and narrowed his eyes. "Are you serious?"

Matt nodded before answering him. "I'm as serious as I've ever been." He raised his left hand up to scratch an itch on his nose before continuing. "A nuclear device was probably detonated high up in the atmosphere and that sent an electromagnetic pulse into the air which destroyed any electronic device with a microchip inside it." He paused but people were still trying to digest what he'd just told them. There were about 100 people inside the town hall of varying ages, and all eyes were locked on him.

Then a small man near the back raised his hand. Matt acknowledged him with a nod.

"Matt, I think I read about this once. Couldn't something like this also be caused by a big solar flare as well?"

"That's correct. That is possible. I'm just assuming it's a nuclear EMP simply because dozens, perhaps hundreds of nuclear bombs have been detonated across the planet during the first week after The Day."

Another man raised his hand and asked a question. "So why didn't this happen on the first day, ya know, when the first bomb fell?"

Matt nodded. "Good question." He made eye contact with the man. "It has to do with the extreme high altitude of the nuclear explosion. The device was probably detonated somewhere between 100 and 200 miles above the earth. A nuclear bomb exploding close to the earth at low altitudes will still create power outages, but they'll be confined to within just a few miles of the blast."

A woman sitting near the front raised her hand. "So how much of the country is without power right now?"

Matt smiled. They were starting to get it. "Good question, but very difficult to answer. It really all depends on how high the bomb detonated and how big the blast was. The higher the altitude and the greater the yield the more widespread the damage will be."

The woman followed up with another question. "So,

what's your best guess?"

Matt paused to think about it, because he really didn't know the answer to her question.

"Probably half the country, the western half, is out of power. Of course, it could be the whole country, but a bomb that large would have had to have been launched from Russia or China or North Korea, and my information tells me those countries lost most of their nuclear capabilities within the first few days of the conflict. So I'm guessing it was a smaller missile that was launched from a container ship off the west coast." He paused before going on. "Of course that doesn't mean that a second missile couldn't have been detonated off the east coast as well, but ... well, the news I've heard is that the east coast cities were hit much harder than the heartland and the west coast."

Then an older man in the front blurted out a question. "Okay, so tell me why my car still runs when everybody else's won't even start?"

Matt nodded. "Is it an older car?"

"Yep. A 1968 Dodge Challenger. I restored it myself."

Matt smiled. "That's good. I think you'll all find that any car or truck with a carburetor instead of fuel injection will probably still work. The bottom line is whether or not there are computer chips and circuit boards inside your vehicles. The older the car, the less electronics it has."

The same man followed up. "So can we modify the cars to bypass the circuitry?"

Matt smiled again. This was taking a turn for the better, and he was starting to understand why Luke Gibbons was so proud of his town.

"Yes, I think so. But you'd need to know about mechanics and electronics. Before The Day, I printed out the directions for doing this, and I can give you a copy." He looked around the room. "I can give copies to anyone who thinks they can do it."

A few of the people started to whisper back and forth, and Matt took this as a good sign. He looked over at Luke Gibbons for direction and he was smiling.

"Are there anymore questions?"

No one raised their hand, so Matt left the front and took his place beside his new wife. Chief of Police Gibbons then walked to the front and motioned with his hands for them to stop talking so they could hear him. They quickly hushed.

"I think what we need to do now folks is to work together on this thing. Every town on the planet is going through the same thing we are, and it's going to be a long, hard winter this year. I can't overstate this folks. If we don't pull together and come up with a very good plan of action, then most of us won't be alive come spring thaw."

Luke pulled up the giant white board on rollers and began to write on it. Across the top he wrote the word "Ideas."

"Let's just have a little brainstorming session. All of you are involved. This is your town, so everyone has to be on board with what we come up with." He paused and looked out among them for several seconds. "What is important to you all? What do you think we should do?"

There was silence for several seconds before a man in the second row raised his hand. "Luke, I don't mean no disrespect, but we were just attacked by some out-of-towners, and you 'n Matt did a good job a killin' 'em, but we still lost some good folks. My question is this. Do ya think that can happen again, and what are we gonna do about it?"

Luke responded right away by writing the word "SECURITY" across the left side of the white board. And then he spoke frankly to them.

"The thing is, folks, I can't protect you anymore. At least not the way I used to. I can't call in the state troopers or the county deputies for help. For the most part I think we're on our own now, and we need to set up a system where every last person can add to the protection of the community."

The man then asked. "How we gonna do that?"

Luke smiled. "Well, I'm glad you asked that question, because I have a few ideas that I'd like to bounce off you." And then he wrote them down on the white board.

1. Expand police reserve.
2. Every adult citizen gets armed and trained.
3. Guard checkpoints at main access roads.
4. Set up comm system.

And then Luke expanded on each point. "I only have three reserve officers with training. I need more. Of course we won't be able to pay you anything, but ... what the heck, there's nothing for you to buy even if you had money, so, problem solved. I'd like enough officers to have two on duty around the clock. Their job would be to keep the peace and to sound the alarm should something bad happen. I'm willing to train whoever volunteers. We should also set up checkpoints at both ends of town to keep out the riff-raff. And I highly recommend all of us start carrying our firearms for added security, at least until we know how bad this thing is going to get." He paused. "And anyone who has a working radio should contact Matt so he can set up a communications system. We need to be able to talk to one another."

A woman off to the side raised her hand. "Are you imposing martial law? Is this gonna be a dictatorship?"

Luke laughed out loud. "No, Martha. Nothing like that. Besides, I know better than to try and control you, cuz you'd kick my ass."

The rest of the room laughed as well and Martha smiled. "I'm glad you recognize that, Luke."

"Martha, everything has to be above boards and in accordance with the constitution. To be honest with you, martial law has already been declared at the federal level, but, to be quite frank, the feds have problems of their own and they won't be able to help or hinder us for quite some time."

And then his voice became serious and his eyes narrowed as he looked out across the crowd. "You folks know me and you know my family. And you know I'm a man of my word. So, I'm giving you my word right now that I will continue to uphold and defend the Bill of Rights. There will be no illegal searches, no confiscation of guns, no one's property will be taken from them by me or anyone working in this town's government. The republic is still alive and well right here in Pigeon Creek, and we'll hold free and fair elections like we always have." He paused. "Any questions so far?"

"So you're not gonna come to my house and take away my food?"

Luke made eye contact with the man directly. "Of course not, Frank. That's against the law, and I'll incarcerate anyone who breaks the law. Nothing has changed in that regard, though we may have to tackle some logistical problems should we run into a crime surge. But listen, folks, I'm proud of this town, and I don't think many of us are going to all of a sudden start stealing from our neighbors. I think our biggest threat will come from the outside, but we can protect against that if we pull together on it."

And then pastor Goodard raised his hand. Luke acknowledged him right away.

"The church has always had a food pantry where we give out food to people in hard times. We plan to keep on doing that for as long as it's needed. So if any of you have extra and want to donate, then we'll make sure it gets to the right people. You have my word on that."

Luke nodded. "Thank you, pastor. I appreciate that. So if anyone has extra, please see Pastor Goodard."

"Any questions or comments." A man raised his hand, and Luke called on him. "Yes, Eric."

"Well, we don't got a mayor right now. He was in Boise when this happened and we haven't heard from him. You mentioned elections. Maybe we should replace him?"

There were murmurs throughout the crowd at this suggestion. Then several others blurted out comments, and Luke shushed them with his hands. "Come on, folks, one at a time. You first Sara."

"I think we should wait to see if he comes back."

"And you, Fred."

"He was a jerk and I never liked him. I say we replace him."

Luke smiled. He'd never been fond of him either, but had shared that with no one but Theresa.

"Mary, you have an opinion?"

The woman stood. "Why don't we schedule an election for 30 days from now? That gives him enough time to get back if he's going to, and we can use that time to organize a fair election."

Luke saw heads nodding up and down across the room, so he went with it.

"So Mary would you like to make a motion that we

hold an election in 30 days?"

"Yes, I would."

"Is there a second?"

"I second it."

Luke smiled. "The motion is carried. We'll hold an election for a new mayor in 30 days, provided Aaron Fields hasn't returned from Boise by then."

He looked over at Esther Williams and asked. "Esther, you're the town clerk, would you like to arrange the details of the election and then present them to us next week so we can all agree on them?"

Esther was a quiet woman, always shy, and seldom voicing her opinion. She was one of those people who did a lot of work, but seldom took the credit for it. She lived alone, a widow for the past 7 years, so she had plenty of time on her hands. She looked around the room and saw everyone staring at her, waiting for her response.

"Umm, yeah. I guess I could do that."

Luke looked out over the room. "Do we need to vote on that or is everyone okay with Esther doing it?"

No one said anything, so Luke moved on. "Well, okay then. That's settled." He looked out over the crowd. "Is there anything else we need to discuss today?"

The room was already buzzing with chatter, but no one else asked to speak, so Luke ended the meeting with little pomp. Then he walked over to Matt and Samantha.

"Well, Matt. What do ya think?"

Matt smiled. "I like it. It's only a start though you know. We have so many things to figure out and not a lot of time before winter sets in."

Luke laughed. "I know. But this town is filled with good people, so I'm not too worried about it. And I have other reasons for my optimism."

Samantha chimed in. "Oh really? And what is that?"

He looked her square in the eye. "Sam, I have every intention of nominating your husband for mayor and doing my best to see that he's elected."

Matt's mouth dropped open and he looked over at Sam, not knowing what to say. Just then several people walked up to Luke and started asking him questions, so the conversation was over, at least for right now.

Another man walked up to Matt and introduced himself. "Hey, Matt. My name's George Fallow and I'd like a copy of them instructions on how to get cars runnin' again. Ya got them on ya?"

Matt gave him a copy, and then noticed that a line of people were waiting to talk to him. He glanced over at Samantha and shrugged. "Honey, do you mind?"

Samantha sighed. "Of course not, honey. I guess that's what I get for marrying such an important man."

Matt turned to field the next question, which was about gathering and preserving food. The next question was about how to get radios working again. After that he talked to a man about reloading ammo. And then another person asked about setting up a generator using a wind turbine.

The questions were unending, and Matt couldn't help but ask himself, *Where were all you people while I was doing my show The Happy Prepper, because that was the best time to prepare.* But he sighed to himself and thought, *Oh well. Better late than never.* And he answered all their questions until late in the afternoon.

But in the back of the room, one man, dirty and disheveled, slipped out the door and into the sunlight. No one talked to him or even seemed to notice him. He quickly walked away and back to the house to report what he'd seen and heard.

*When Abram heard that his relative had
been taken captive, he called out the 318
trained men born in his household and went
in pursuit as far as Dan.*

Genesis 14:14 (NIV)

CHAPTER 20

10 miles inside Idaho

THE NEXT MORNING, MARVE opened his eyes, but couldn't see, and that scared him. He called out to Alex, but she didn't answer him. His head was throbbing with the worst pain of his life and he could barely move. He managed to reach his right hand over and check his wife's sleeping bag, but she wasn't there. He called out to her.

"Alex! I can't see!" But there was no answer. He tried to sit up, but the pain wouldn't let him, and he almost passed out. He called out again. "Alex! Are you there! I need you. Help me."

As he lay there in pain and all alone, he could hear birds singing in the field around him. Then he heard a cow moo off in the distance. And then Marvin began to cry, not really knowing why, just knowing that something terrible must have happened and he didn't know what it was. The tears moistened his eyes and softened the blood that had dried and kept his eyelids from opening. At first his sight was pink and blurry, but then, as he blinked them open and shut, his eyesight began to return.

Once his eyesight was back, he slowly turned his head to one side and saw his wife's empty sleeping bag. There were drag marks on the ground, and her Marine Corps baseball cap was on the ground a few feet away. He remembered that Sergeant Major Stafford had given it to her as a parting gift. She'd been so proud of it.

Marvin tried to roll over, but pain shot all throughout his rib cage, forcing him to lay still for a while. As he lie there, he tried to calm himself down and think rationally. What had happened? He had no conscious knowledge of what had transpired in the night. The last he remembered was thinking that he should set up a watch, but was just too tired to follow through with it. He regretted that now.

And then he thought about Alex. Someone must've taken her. He forced his broken body to roll over on his belly, and then he bent his legs up so he could get his head up out of the dirt. He reached down to his waist ad fumbled for his pistol, but it wasn't there. They must've taken it. And then he felt something hard and sharp digging into his left knee, so he reached down and felt the object. It was his Glock 19. He picked it up and tried to put it back in his appendix holster and was successful after three attempts.

He took a few seconds to look around him now, and saw horse tracks in the dirt. The fire was still smoldering, just a tiny wisp of smoke that he could still smell. And then Marvin began to cry like a grieving child. He wailed out loud so hard that it made his chest hurt. After a few minutes he stopped, and the grief was replaced with rage.

They had stolen his wife. He loved her, and he knew she was suffering. Marvin knew what type of heinous things they'd be doing to her, but he pushed those thoughts down into a different part of his brain, putting them in a box where he could access them later when he had more time.

But what to do now? That was the only question that mattered. He had to save her. But how? He didn't know where she was. Marvin dug his right hand into the dry sand, then lifted it up off the ground and let it trickle through his fingertips.

And then, suddenly, he remembered Will Stafford's footlocker. With a sheer force of will, Marvin forced himself up onto his feet. The pain was almost overwhelming, but his time in the Marines came back to him now, reminding him of who he was and all he'd accomplished in life. As a young Marine, he'd been taught that he could do anything, so he latched onto those twenty-year-old teachings and looked around him. His head still throbbed, but his vision had cleared. He saw the entrenching tool where they'd left it the night before, and hobbled slowly over to get it.

It was painful to reach down that far, but he did it anyway. Then he walked slowly into the field where he thought the trunk was buried. It took five minutes to find the slight mound of unsettled soil, and then he began to dig. The going was painfully slow, and it took his a full hour to uncover it. Marvin tried to lift it out, but screamed in pain before stopping. In the end, he decided to just unlatch it and open the lid. On the top were the Claymore mines, the LAW and the body armor. He gently lifted them out slowly, one at a time and laid them on the ground beside him. He dug around inside the trunk, moving aside magazines and dehydrated food and even a pair of night vision goggles.

And then he saw what he needed. It was a small box ... a portable Faraday cage. He lifted it out and set it on the ground beside him. With a good deal of effort he opened the lid and looked inside. He smiled when he saw the handheld shortwave transceiver. There was a handwritten note on top that read "My frequency is programmed in. Just turn on the power and talk! Semper Fi!"

Marvin smiled and lifted the radio out of the Faraday cage. He saw the power button and turned it on. It immediately thrummed to life. At first he heard static, but then it cleared. He pressed the button to talk.

"Sergeant Major, this is Sergeant Tubbs, over."

He waited several seconds for a response, but none came, so he tried again.

"Sergeant Major Will Stafford, this is Sergeant Marvin Tubbs. This is an emergency. Come in, over."

But there was still no response. Marvin realized that it could take a while to connect with Will, simply because he'd have to be monitoring the radio in his basement command post for him to hear Marvin's transmission. Or, it could be that he was out of range. Then he looked down and saw the coil of wire also in the box, and he remembered his military training. He uncoiled the wire and attached one end to the antennae, then he spread the wire out as far as it would go on the ground. Hanging it up in a tree would be better, but Marvin just wasn't capable of doing that right now. He tried transmitting again.

"Sergeant Major Will Stafford, this is Sergeant Marvin Tubbs. This is an emergency. Come in, over."

He waited, but nothing but silence came back at him

"Sergeant Major Will Stafford, this is Sergeant Marvin Tubbs. This is an emergency. Come in, over."

Marvin dropped the radio down into the box and swore out loud. Then he heard a bit of static come and go quickly. He reached down and picked up the radio again.

"Sergeant Major, this is Sergeant Tubbs. This is an emergency. Come in, over."

A flood of relief came over Marvin when he heard a voice through the tiny speaker.

"Good morning, Marine. What can I do ya for?"

Marvin smiled despite all the pain.

"I need help, Will. I'm in dire straits."

There was a pause.

"Give me a sit rep, over."

"We were attacked last night. They have Alex. I'm badly hurt. I need help to get her back. Over."

The response was quick.

"What is your location, over."

Marvin thought about that for a few seconds. He wasn't exactly sure where he was. Then he remembered the last road sign.

"I'm about 10 miles inside Idaho. It's a secondary road called Umatilla. Can you help, over?"

"Roger that, Marine. I see you on the map now. It's about a 3-hour drive. I'll be there in two. Can you hold on, over?"

Marvin was so relieved that he wanted to cry again, but he didn't.

"Roger that, Sergeant Major. I'll be waiting."

He paused. "And ... thank you, sir."

When Will answered, Marvin could hear laughter on the line. "Don't call me sir or I'll kick your ass! I ain't no officer! Now just shut up and don't do anything stupid before I get there. Gotta go. I got clicks to turn. Over and out."

And then the line went silent again. His thoughts went immediately to his wife and he worried about her, wondering ... what are they doing to her? Was she even still alive. And then a thought came to him. *Maybe I should pray for her?*

He bowed his head and folded his hands.

"Lord God almighty. Please be with Alex. Please protect her until I can get there. Please ..."

But his words were interrupted by a sound off in the distance. It was a creaking noise, and then he heard a horse whinny. He hid down behind some brush and peeked out just in time to see a horse-drawn wagon with two men in front. Both were carrying rifles.

Alexandra's Plight

SHE WOKE UP SLOWLY, BARELY ABLE TO MOVE, NOT knowing where she was or how she got there. Alexandra's head felt heavy, like it was filled with sand, making it difficult for her to figure things out, so she spent the next few minutes in the dark just thinking. The last thing she could remember was waking up while being drug from her sleeping bag beside Marvin. She remembered them beating and kicking her husband as they pulled her away. She'd tried to get a good look at him as they were dragging her off, but it had been hard seeing in the dark. But Alex was worried. Marve hadn't moved at all, and that wasn't like him. Marve would have fought to his dying breath to save her, but ... he hadn't moved. Was he dead?

She pushed the idea out of her head. She refused to believe that. She couldn't believe that. After all, Marvin was her only hope of rescue. In the silent darkness, she found herself praying to a God she hardly knew. "Please

God. Protect my husband. Show him where I am. Please God. Save me."

Just then, she heard a door open and the sound of footsteps on a hard floor. She opened her eyes but all she saw was black. Then she felt a hand on the back of her head; it was untying something. A moment later the blindfold was ripped from her head and a million lights ripped into her brain. She blinked repeatedly as strong arms picked her up and placed her on a chair. Her hands were bound behind her back, and she heard and felt a roll of duct tape being wrapped around her torso.

Finally, her eyes adjusted to the light, and she saw a man sitting in a chair across from her. He was smiling, but it wasn't a happy smile; it was the kind of smile someone made right before tearing the wings off a fly. She shuddered.

"Where is my husband?"

The man crossed his arms across his chest. He was strong, well-built, and about 45 years old. He wore a beard that extended several inches down past his chin.

"He's dead. We beat him to death."

And then he said nothing, just watched her reaction. Alex wanted to launch herself at him, to scream in defiance and deny his statement, but ... in her heart, she had a feeling it was true; that Marvin really was dead. After all, that agreed with what she'd seen.

"Let me go."

The man didn't say anything at first. He just stared at her, and that drove Alex crazy. She yelled as loud as she could.

"I said let me go you piece of ...!"

But she never got a chance to finish the sentence. She didn't know how, but the man jumped up, stepped forward, all in one fluid motion and hit her with the back of his hand as hard as he could. Her head jerked off to the right, and the only thing holding her to the chair was the duct tape. When she looked up, he was already seated.

Alex tasted the blood inside her mouth but said nothing. He still stared at her, the smile gone now, just looking at her, devoid of all emotion. He crossed his arms across his chest again.

"You will learn to keep a civil tongue. Obedience will be rewarded. Disobedience will be punished." He glanced past her and out the window behind her. His attention was focused some where else for just a few seconds, then his eyes locked back onto her like a laser. "It's okay. You're not helpless. You are in total control of your words and your actions." He paused. "You may say anything you want and do anything you want."

Alex looked at him sceptically while cocking her head to one side. "So, if I want, then I can call you a dirty, rotten ..." The moment he stood and moved toward her, Alex closed her mouth and waited for the blow. But ... it never came. He smiled as he sat back down.

"You're smarter than the others." His smile broadened. "Hot and feisty, but you learn quickly." Her captor glanced over to the man standing beside the door and nodded his head. The other man was very big, but he left the room immediately. The boss looked back at her.

"The rules are simple. You are free, except for those ropes on your hands, but that won't last forever. Your success and pleasure here with us is totally up to you. You have control. You will decide your own fate ... whether you live ... or whether you die." His smile vanished. "Do you understand me?"

Alex didn't say anything. She simply nodded her head

slowly and compliantly. The man suddenly stood and towered over her as he spoke.

"My men will now give you a bath and get you cleaned up for me."

He recognized the look of fear spread across her face. "Don't worry. They won't hurt you unless you give them reason." He turned and walked toward the door. He stopped and turned upon reaching it.

"I'm saving you for myself. You don't realize it yet, but ... that's an honor." And then he turned one last time and walked out the door.

When the door was completely shut, Alex let her head drop down onto her chest. She cried out loud softly, so no one outside the door could hear her.

"Marvin, please. I'm here. I love you honey. Please come save me."

But for all she knew, her husband was dead.

Here ends book 2 of *The Mad American*, but there are many more challenges to face and more dangers to overcome for Matt, Samantha, Marv and Alex in this new apocalyptic world. Thank you so much for reading my story.

Please do me a favor now and write a positive review and put it on Amazon. That really does help with sales. Also, please tell your friends about the book via social networking.

And now, I'll get busy writing book 3 in the series. It's coming soon!

Skip Coryell lives with his wife and children in Michigan. He works full time as a professional writer, and *The Mad American: Day of Reckoning* is his 21st published book. He is an avid hunter and sportsman, a Marine Corps veteran, and a graduate of Cornerstone University. You can listen to Skip as he co-hosts the syndicated military talk radio show *Frontlines of Freedom* on frontlinesoffreedom.com. You can also hear his weekly podcast *The Home Defense Show* at homedefenseshow.com.

For more details on Skip Coryell, or to contact him personally, go to his website at skipcoryell.com

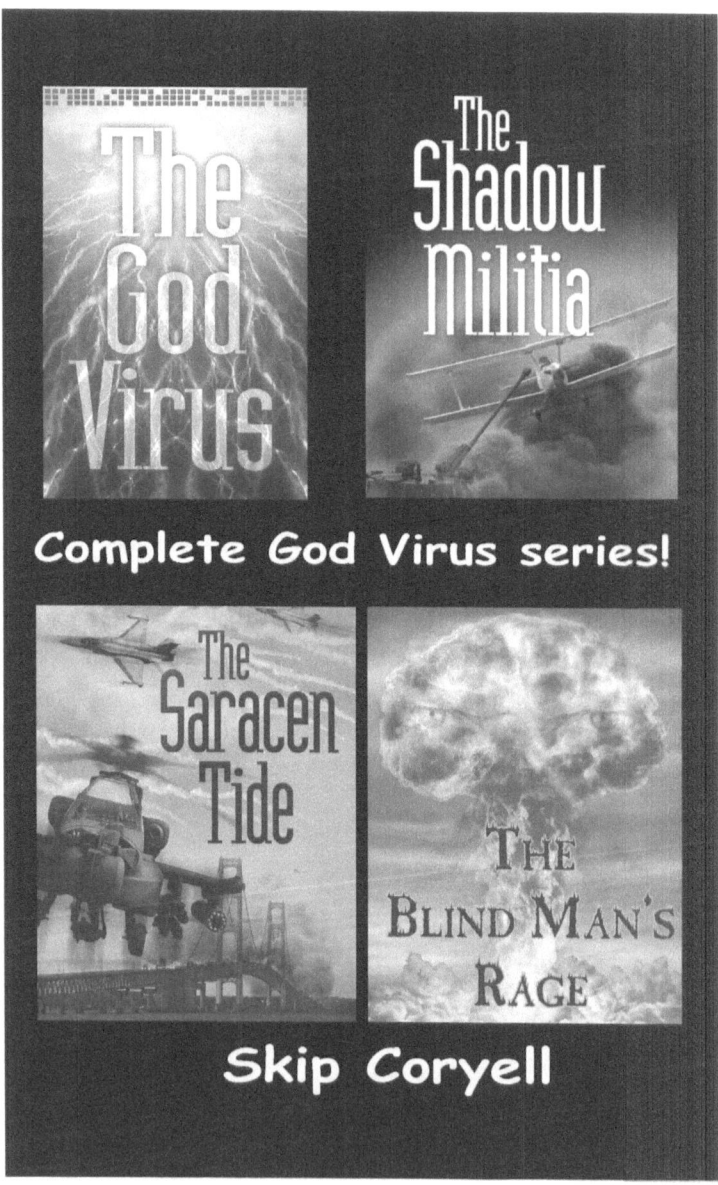

This is 4 books in one! The complete 4-book God Virus apocalyptic adventure series beneath one cover. Suddenly, the lights went out, not just in one town or village, but all across the world. It was an act of cyber terrorism that plunged the world into the heart of darkness, into the 1000-year night, letting loose the demons of a billion souls, pitting dark against light, causing each person everywhere to choose sides. Not since Stephen King's "The Stand" has there been an apocalyptic thriller of such epic proportions. Read the entire 4-book series and see what happens when society's thin veneer of civility is stripped away. "The God Virus" series is gripping, seething and oozing with the best and worst humanity has to offer.

SKIP CORYELL

CONCEALED CARRY *for* **CHRISTIANS**

I started carrying a pistol over 20 years ago, and I've been a member of a church safety team for just as long. The church safety team is like other ministries in that we are serving the body of Christ, but there is one very distinct and important difference. It might get you killed.

I've been a Sunday school teacher, even Sunday School Superintendent. I've served on musical teams. I've been an usher. I've even helped in the children's ministry where they expected me to dance up and down to silly songs while making ridiculous hand motions. (Thank God there are no existing pictures for that one. It wasn't pretty.)

However, none of those jobs ever required me to take a bullet for the flock. As a Sunday School teacher, I was never expected to run towards gunshots while drawing my firearm. Most Sunday School teachers don't carry pepper spray; they don't practice open-handed skills to become proficient at taking a man to the ground and putting him in zip ties. They are not trained in the subtle arts of interrogation and visually identifying physical threats, like who is armed and who is not.

It's a different kind of ministry, requiring a different kind of Christian. However, all these concerns are not restricted to the church safety team, because they apply to any Christian who decides to carry a gun.

If you are considering carrying a gun or joining a church safety team, then, this book is a must-listen for you. You should not go into the job lightly, as there are many things to consider. Can you take a human life? Killing a fellow human being is not and should not be a natural and easy thing to do. It should be tough. It may take years of prayer and study and self-reflection before you decide the answer. Do you want to carry a gun? It's a nuisance, a total life change, and a bona fide pain in the butt. Carrying a gun dictates every facet of your life: how you treat others, what you wear, how you talk, and how you walk. It's not for everyone.

Are you willing to die to protect the ones you love? How about strangers? Will you die to protect someone you haven't even met yet. Are you willing to spend lots of time and money on training and equipment? Less than one percent of the concealed carry population ever go on to take training that is not required by the government. That statistic should scare you.

Buying a gun doesn't make you a gun fighter any more than buying a guitar makes you a rock star. We are called by God to excellence in everything we do. The gun is a powerful tool. The sacrifice you make could be supreme. It is a life-or-death decision. This book was written to empower and encourage Christians who decide to carry concealed. You are an elite corps of individuals. You are warriors. Welcome to the club! - Skip Coryell

If masculinity is toxic, then Jack Ruger is the cultural equivalent of a raging bull on steroids. Born and raised in the cold and frozen northern paradise of Michigan's upper peninsula, Chief of Police Jack Ruger is sworn to protect and defend the citizens of Jackpine. So when escaped killer Bobby Lee Harper descends on the town, threatening to kill him and all he holds dear, it's a formal declaration of war, and only one man will survive.

More and more people across the country are seeing the dangers in society and deciding to carry concealed to protect themselves and their families. Skip's book lays it out step by step, teaching you how to protect and defend the ones you love. Read his book and get the benefit of his 20+ years of teaching experience and his lifetime of training for this important role in society. *Civilian Combat* is also a great teaching tool for other concealed carry instructors as well. It's a complete curriculum with a final test as well as important points to remember and a list of excellent resources in your journey to personal and family protection.

Skip is the creator and host of *The Home Defense Show*, a weekly 1-hour podcast about all things home, family and personal defense.

The Home Defense Show podcast is now available on iTunes, iHeart, Google Play, Spreaker and Sticher. You can also find it on my YouTube channel. This should make it easier than ever for you to listen to my sweet angelic voice coming to you from deep inside the bowels of a great big empty. Don't forget to subscribe.

For more info go to homedefenseshow.com

FRONTLINES OF FREEDOM RADIO

You can hear authors Denny Gillem and Skip Coryell on one of your local stations on the number 1 military talk show in America. *Frontlines of Freedom* is syndicated on over 180 stations, and is also available as a podcast on frontlinesoffreedom.com.

Books by Skip Coryell

We Hold These Truths
Bond of Unseen Blood
Church and State
Blood in the Streets
Laughter and Tears
RKBA: Defending the Right to Keep and Bear Arms
Stalking Natalie
The God Virus
The Shadow Militia
The Saracen Tide
The Blind Man's Rage
Civilian Combat - The Concealed Carry Book
Jackpine Strong
Concealed Carry for Christians
The Covid Chronicles: Surviving the Upgrade
The Covid Chronicles: Surviving the Apocalypse
The Covid Chronicles: Surviving the Solstice
The Mad American - Judgment Day
The Mad American - Day of Reckoning
Sunrise Reflections: Finding Hope in Hard Times
Self Defense Scenarios: Staying Alive in a
Dangerous World

www.ingramcontent.com/pod-product-compliance
Lightning Source LLC
Chambersburg PA
CBHW050520260626

47157CB00004B/1405